Mairzy Doats

Glory Fagan

I know a ditty nutty as a fruitcake

Goofy as a goon and silly as a loon

Some call it pretty, others call it crazy

But they all sing this tune:

Mairzy doats and dozy doats and liddle lamzy divey

A kiddley divey too, wouldn't you?

Yes! Mairzy doats and dozy doats and liddle lamzy divey

A kiddley divey too, wouldn't you?

If the words sound queer and funny in your ear, a little bit jumbled and jivey

Sing, "Mares eat oats and does eat oats and little lambs eat ivy."

A kiddley divey too, wouldn't you?

~The Pied Pipers

This is entirely a work of fiction. But at the heart lies an intersection of true stories told by unreliable narrators.

Mairzy Doats by Glory Fagan

Title taken from lyric "Mairzy Doats" written and composed by Milton Drake, Al Hoffman, and Jerry Livingstone. An alternate spelling, "Mairzy Doates," refers to an American thoroughbred racehorse named for the novelty song.

Cover by Glory Fagan

Now

I would have turned 100 today, if I'd lived. You would be right to reckon I'm dead. Have been for a number of years. News of my death will come as no surprise to those who'll remember me, but the fact that I am still at it and might have something to say will. Surprises me a little. Figured I'd just evaporate into nothingness upon dying. Zane will take reading this the hardest but will be most pleased. She prefers realism in books and takes her Bible most to heart. It's like she wants her fiction to be true and her truth to be miraculous. That woman knows and loves Jesus. Unlike Mother who brandished fundamentalism like the torch she often carried in the dark. Mother never saw the irony of holding a light while hiding behind robes. Mother knew her Old Testament forward and back but never set foot in the New.

If my Dad were still alive, he might jot a note on the

significance of today's date in his journal. "D-- helped plow

the north 10 acres. BIG NEWS. D---turned 100. Left this

mortal earth 20 years ago. Must have converted after all.

Praise be to God. Husked corn. Attended school meeting in

the p.m. Paid the phone rent, $4.67." Dad died shortly before

Zane was born, so he might find it humorous that people still

rent phones. Then there'd be Johnnie. He had a way of

hedging his bets. He laid odds on his own theological angle

running the table, so he wouldn't be a bit surprised that I'm

still around.

Mainly word of my continued existence won't square neatly

with Mother's idea of divine retribution or Zane's hope of

salvation. Zane was always concerned with my mortal

happiness and my immortal destination. Mother will be

chagrined I've not yet been consigned to flames. She has no

idea I spent my life repenting. Daddy's hope was always that

I'd fall on my knees at the altar so that when I passed out of

this life, I would be admitted into the next. Zane just prayed that I share in her blessed assurance and find peace. None of this lines up with their either-or worldview. Like I said, Johnnie is rarely caught off guard. He lost me when he gambled his life away, but if I saw him again, he'd probably just say my voice had changed. Even I notice that. What surprises me is that he's the husband who should come to mind. Maybe it's because my first husband worked out his own unorthodox salvation. I spent so much energy forgetting my next husband and even now try so hard to hang on to memories of the last, the truest love of my life.

I suppose some might call this state I'm in purgatory, but I am not sure what all that would entail. Despite lifelong sincere attempts by others, I never really settled on a religion. Moderation was the one virtue I espoused. When you live among extremes, you develop an affinity for all things in moderation. Suffice it to say, one day I died, but I for some reason I don't seem all that dead. I have no way of knowing whether this is the fate of all who are deceased, or if

5

I'm special. Wouldn't that be a hoot?

Since receiving "seminiscience," that's the way I see it, a semi-omniscience, I am able to see things with a clarity never afforded me in life. Even I don't fully understand the mechanics. I regret I have lost touch with those I left behind in life, but at least they don't have to worry--we don't get any live gossip here. I only just now know my own secrets. No use spending too much time trying to understand how any of this is possible. Just listen in to what I have to say, if you've a mind to.

And here's another thing. This might be even more startling. I may have been born a century ago, but now it's like I'm every age at once. Growing up on the farm, helping Dad, avoiding Mother, leaving Nebraska for Chicago at 18. It's all going on at the same time, good, bad, lonesome, happy. I am alone with Zane in the apartment while Johnnie is overseas with the army. Finding out Daddy died. Seeing Zane all

6

grown up. The grandkids being born. These aren't memories,
but part of who I am now. I can't rightly explain it. There is
only that one time, that void, and I'm ever so grateful not to
be able to see into it.

I think it's possible that Zane would actually understand this
part. I hear her prayers and sometimes get glimpses of her
dreams. Shortly after my death, she dreamed that the me who
had just died met the young me in an office. She was so
happy to make the introduction, and I overheard her
thanking God for that little nocturnal reassurance. I know
this because sometimes her mind strays as she's talking to
the Almighty. When that happens, I wade into currents of her
consciousness. That's how I found out about the dream. She
was praying after I died, counting her dream where I was
both young and old as a blessing. She took it as a sign I was
going to be okay.

One time I saw the stage play Our Town. At the end, people
in a graveyard talked. But dead people talking wasn't the

7

part that really stuck with me. There was this man who

seemed to know all about those townspeople's beginnings

and endings. I wondered if he knew about his own? At the

time, I didn't see how any of it was possible. Well, these days

I, too, like my entertainment to be a little bit real and a whole

lot far-fetched. Guess knowing now about others makes me a

Stage Manager. Even though that Stage Manager was just

the creation of the playwright Thornton Wilder, he is as real

as you or me. Still I bet that show had to have had another

actual stage manager on top of the capitalized one. I also feel

a little like those citizens in the cemetery, talking about the

weather and goings on about town long after they were too

dead for such concerns. Like them, Daddy and Mother will

get their say in this book. So will I.

Twenty years ago, give or take, I sloughed off the old mortal

coil, and I've been hanging around ever since. I don't know if

this is what forever holds, or if I'm just doing time in some

type of limbo, so I best be getting on with telling my side of things in case there is a life after this one. At first, I was just taking it all in myself. I know full well Mother will be upset knowing I escaped perdition. Not that she wanted me to end up tormented in brimstone, but she thought that was where I was bound if I didn't clean up my act, close that 18-inch gap between head knowledge and heart belief. She'll think I cheated somehow, didn't play by the rules. Zane will be perplexed but relieved. She really wanted me to find redemption. Dad died so young, but he hoped to see all his kiddies, that's what he called us, again when the roll is called up yonder. Time will tell.

So here's how I see it. No one need take just my word for it. Besides any records I kept are long gone. Before I died, I asked Lew to burn my words when I was gone. Every one of them. Notebooks and notebooks of words. Like Dad, I kept accounts. Dad recorded everything in his journal, Mother scribbled her infernal letters, and Zane prayed. I kept a meticulous account but decided I didn't want anybody else

9

reading it. This is my chance to tell my side of things. I have

some more perspective now. My intention is not to go all

Jacob Marley on anyone. I saw that picture show, too. I

won't presume to fix anyone else's life when it's so well

documented that I made a mess of my own.

Spring 1955

Wheeled from the surgery theater back to her room, she

struggled to open her eyes. Pushed by unseen hands, the

gurney coursed through the halls of the institution once

officially known as State Hospital for the Insane #2. Long

renamed St. Joseph State Hospital for less ominous

connotation, the facility continued to house within its

labyrinthian walls those battling clinical depression

alongside the criminally insane. Patients were treated

equally, the former ostensibly for their own good and the

latter more often than not for the benefit of the staff. Here

egalitarian currents of electroconvulsive shock were

routinely transmitted with great effect to produce wraiths incapable of resistance. Those diagnosed with a nervous breakdown encountered further reduction by electrically-induced compliance.

Inattentive attendants cursed the arrhythmia of wheels out of sync that sent the stretcher into a cart, knocking a metal tray to the tile floor with a clatter echoed by a tourette of expletives erupting from the dining hall. Still the echo chamber of her own breathing and the staccato of her beating heart stifled any bedlam beyond her senses. Vague wakefulness recalled her body's earlier attempt at instinctive fight, a thrashing subsided only with the application of restraints. Now harsh light emanating from the ceiling ballasts worked against her efforts to find asylum in the darkness behind lidded eyes. Unable to put up a struggle against the oppressive weight of exhaustion, she succumbed as orderlies moved her once restive body back into her bed.

Minutes passed. She roused somewhat and willed herself to think. Think. Certain they had gone, she forced herself to open one eye cautiously. Relieved that Matron was not in the small room and that the curtains had been drawn, concealing the catatonic woman in the other bed, she fought inertia to lift her head. Summoning the strength remaining in her slender arms, she attempted to sit upright, resting halfway on her elbows.

The nightstand was on her left. Her right hand crossed her body, but the drawer remained just out of reach. Shifting back into the bed, she caught her breath before trying again, this time with her left arm. Grasping the bed rail with her right hand to anchor her slight weight, she listed leeward until her pinky and ringless ring finger caught the drawer handle. Painfully, with two hooked fingers, she pulled the wheeled set of drawers slightly closer.

The sudden sight of a partially shaved head atop the stand caused her to lose contact with the handle. Darkly circled eyes reflected in the shined steel surface of an institutional mirror atop the nightstand stared back at her. Vague recognition dawned, making it all the more important to try again. To remember.

Gathering her strength once more, she reached for the drawer, pulling it open a few inches, enough to reach in to retrieve a small book. She opened the little Gideon-issued Bible to The Revelation. There it was. With relief she read a slip of paper upon which were written two words, in a surprisingly even and lovely script. Her name and that of her eleven-year old daughter.

December 1955

Relieved to be one of only a few riders, Zane took the nearest empty seat and slid across the bench to the window. She placed her red plaid school satchel in the seat to discourage anyone from taking a seat. The satchel contained a wrapped present and a sketch pad. Zane didn't know the exact address, but she knew she would be able to see the hospital from the city bus. She had taken this route before.

She looked down on the sidewalks passing beneath her, her breath fogging the glass. With a gloved finger, she drew the outline of a dog, her spaniel Nosie, in the condensation. A little black Cocker with brown markings, Nosie was the one constant in her life, even sleeping with her on the bed since Momma had been away this time.

She had just gotten Momma back and now she was gone again. Momma had seemed so happy there for a while. One day Momma had just shown up unannounced at Aunt Dot and Uncle Hal's farm in Wisconsin to pick her up. Not a single visit or letter or phone call had punctured her long absence. But there Momma was, surprising Zane with a puppy and a new stepfather. The puppy was not only a present; he was a peace offering. Zane had giggled as the puppy wriggled with delight, licking her ears and nestling his muzzle into her neck. The stepfather was Momma's promise to her sister Dorothy that Momma would be able to take care of Zane now. The new little family even had a new house with a steep terrace back in St. Joe. Promises, it turned out, aren't as easily kept as made.

Once they arrived home in Missouri at the new house on Hawthorne with the steep terrace, Momma's rule was that Nosie had to stay on the linoleum and would never be permitted on the furniture. Zane sighed, refogging the bus window at the memory. She hoped Momma might not mind so much that Nosie slept on her bed under the circumstances. For those first few days after Momma had gone away, Zane had enforced Momma's wishes. The dog stayed in the kitchen but whined at night. As the weeks wore on, Zane's resistance wore off. Nosie offered comfort and companionship through the long nights in the house with the steep terrace.

Zane dotted a nose with her finger on the foggy dog on the bus window. The past few Saturdays, Zane had taken the bus downtown to the hospital. At eleven, she was too young to be admitted as a visitor. Only those 16 and older could visit, but she tried anyway. She knew she would never pass for a teenager, so if she couldn't wear down the resistance of the man at the desk, maybe she could time her arrival when he was away from the desk at lunch. Then she could sneak upstairs and find Momma's room and give Momma her Christmas present.

Zane added spots on the drawing where Nosie had light brown patches. A wave of panic came over Zane as she considered, not for the first time, what would happen if Momma wasn't discharged soon. Momma wouldn't be able to keep her promise. If Momma lost her job, they would lose the house. Zane knew that in all likelihood, Momma had already been fired; they just didn't know it. Mr. Allison, Bob, wouldn't feel obligated to keep Momma on much longer if she never showed up.

Zane had just gotten used to having a stepfather when he suddenly returned to being Mr. Allison again, no longer a figure in their household on Hawthorne. Another pretty lady in the secretarial pool had caught his eye. The muffled arguments behind walls had led to slamming doors. Then it was just the three of them, Momma, Zane, and Nosie. Mr. Allison had agreed to let his ex-wife, his third, continue to work in the office if she didn't make a fuss. He couldn't afford more alimony. He had allowed her to assume the mortgage because she had a daughter to house. Mr. Allison fancied himself a fair-minded man who realized her need for an income. Zane thought him merely self-serving and doubted he could be trusted to keep his word. If Momma didn't have a job, they wouldn't be able to keep the house. If they lost the house, they wouldn't be able to keep Nosie.

17

As far as Zane was concerned, besides getting Momma back, Nosie and the house were the only good things to come out of Momma and Mr. Allison's brief marriage. Zane suddenly realized he had been responsible both for her getting Momma back and for her losing Momma again. Nosie had come from his sister's litter of pups, but since the dog had been free, Mr. Allison could hardly be credited with that. More than anything though, his leaving seemed to be the reason Momma was in the hospital now, so Zane hated him.

Dew ran down the pane, making the picture of the dog look as if it were crying. Zane swiped the image away and turned to face the front. The bus slowed to a stop and a man wearing a fedora carried a small child on board. The child appeared to be a girl, but Zane couldn't be certain. The man's hat made him look a little like Uncle Hal. She wondered briefly if Uncle Hal would still be considered her uncle if he and Aunt Dot were divorced. Men, Uncle Hal, Mr. Allison, and even

18

her Daddy, brought only heartache and trouble. Then and there, Zane decided she was never ever going to marry.

Zane saw the imposing brick edifice of the hospital come into view. The bus slowed to a stop and she reached for her satchel.

Zane approached the heavy hospital doors, pausing under the gaze of a stone Mary and baby Jesus. His birthday would be tomorrow, she realized. She swung the red satchel over her shoulder, took a deep breath, and entered the vestibule. Instead of the uniformed man she had seen on earlier occasions, a woman sat at the desk. Not sure of her next move, Zane took a seat in a straight-back chair under a wooden crucifix in the waiting area, placing the satchel next to her. Out of custom she left two empty seats along the wall separating her from an old man dozing nearby. From early childhood, Zane had enjoyed the company of a trio of imaginary playmates. Too old for such foolishness now, still

19

she left room for Obeob, Okeob, and Mountainary as had
been her habit.

Made up friends with made up names had attended her from
earliest youth in the Chicago apartment she had shared with
Momma while Daddy was overseas during the War. When
Daddy came back, the long-hoped for happy reunion had
been short-lived. Although he took a job at U.S. Steel, Daddy
spent most of his time at the race track. One time he lost on
the ponies, and it cost Momma dearly, wiping out all the
money she had saved toward a house. Another time, the car
was gone. For a time, Momma and Daddy tried to keep Zane
from hearing them argue. Then Daddy wasn't around to fight.
Momma was sad, so Zane took to playing with Obeob,
Okeob, and Mountainary.

"May I help you?" the woman asked, breaking into her
reverie.

"I'm just waiting for my Daddy," Zane answered off the cuff. She left it at that, not having decided whether she was waiting for her Daddy to exit the elevator or for him to arrive. In truth, she had no idea where Daddy might be. His letters were postmarked Chicago. Last time she had seen him was during the summer when he had visited her at the farm. Zane hoped the woman wouldn't further inquire as to his whereabouts. To avoid interaction, Zane withdrew a sketch pad and a sharpened Number 2 pencil from her plaid satchel. Life had taught her to be patient, so she would wait until the woman left the desk.

At eleven years old, Zane was long accustomed to living quietly in her imagination. Drawing always offered escape. Miraculously, one time when she was five, she had found an entire ream of typing paper out by the blacktop that fronted her aunt and uncle's farm where she had been taken without explanation to live. She had spread the damp pages by furnace ducts throughout the house to dry. The 500 images that filled those pages brightened her quiet existence over the next few years.

In the waiting area, Zane drew two curved lines. The outline of a carriage soon floated atop the lines. Ornate brackets connected the carriage to the lined runners, and a horse-drawn sleigh emerged in black and white. Zane remembered seeing the sleigh, green with red pinstripes, hanging from the rafters in the detached garage at the farm where she had gone to live with Aunt Dot and Uncle Hal. She had spent hours in the dusty loft above the garage, playing tea party with Obeob, Okeob, and Mountainary, who had come with her from Chicago, pouring them walnut stained water into chipped dishes.

Assessing the sled's progress on the page, Zane envisioned a ride across the snowy Wisconsin landscape, regretting there had never been anyone around to bring the sleigh down and put it to use. She sketched a barn worthy of Currier and Ives in the background.

That was the first time Momma went away. Her absence had lasted three years, more than a third of Zane's life. One day Zane found herself whisked away from Chicago to a farm in Walworth County, Wisconsin. Her removal was intended to spare her the ugliness of her parents' divorce, but Zane found herself in the care of her mother's sister Dorothy, Aunt Dot, who was enduring struggles of her own. One of Momma's four sisters, Aunt Dot lived on a once flourishing farm surrounded by her family. But months earlier, Zane's cousin Joy had been killed by a car which struck her as she checked the mail. Joy's older brother Roger, angry at the world, had quit high school and run away from home. Mere days before Zane's arrival, a devastating fire burned a newly built horse barn to the ground, killing livestock. Zane remembered wisps of smoke rising from the smoldering ashes of emotional and financial ruin as she took up residence in the room left empty by Roger's vacancy. Shortly after Zane moved in, her aunt

23

discovered her husband Hal had been unfaithful and he, too, moved out. It was into this landscape that Zane had been sent for sanctuary. Of course, Zane did not understand all that at the time. She was only five. Now she was eleven.

For the few years Zane lived with her, Aunt Dot proved a fragile, distant, frugal woman who wanted nothing more than privacy. She did whatever was necessary to care for Zane, but without the comfort of conversation. Zane spent what would have been her kindergarten year, for rural Wisconsin schools offered no such educational luxuries, through second grade in the company of her solitary aunt. Aunt Dot had accepted the responsibility for her sister's child on the condition the girl's mother did not contact them. Momma later explained that Aunt Dot thought the separation would be easier without the disruption of letters, calls, gifts, or visits from her.

During the interim they had no idea what Momma might be

up to, presumably getting her life back together, and since

Momma remained out of contact as agreed, she had no idea

she had unwittingly spared her daughter the trauma of her

own divorce only to drop Zane at the center of the

disintegration of a family of strangers. One morning Uncle

Hal was gone, and Aunt Dot was left to work the farm alone.

No friends or neighbors came with comfort or aid. Aunt Dot,

like Momma, had never returned to church after leaving their

strict Methodist upbringing, so she had no spiritual support.

Her life, alone except for her young niece, provoked only

pity, gossip, and slander.

Zane recalled being called to the principal's office to answer

for their life on the farm. She could only answer, "I don't

know" to questions beyond her scope. Why she was living

there if her name was not the same as her aunt's? Where had

her uncle and cousin Roger gone? Who was the man living

there now?

The summer before Momma came to retrieve her, Daddy had come to visit. He came to see Zane, but seeing the need, had stayed on to help around his former sister-in-law's farm, a move that benefited the three of them equally.

"Do you expect your father shortly?" Zane looked up to find the receptionist smiling at her. She looked at the three empty chairs, one holding her satchel, and answered, smiling sweetly, "I expect he'll be here presently. He just had to drop off my brothers and sister." Then she turned to a fresh page in her sketchbook.

On the new sheet of paper from her sketch pad, Zane outlined a cartoon robe from which Mickey Mouse emerged, wearing a tall, pointed, brimmed hat. She added a crescent moon and stars. Next, she drew a broomstick with arms balancing wooden buckets. She replicated the image, each time tipping the buckets a little more until droplets of water sloshed onto an unseen floor. In her mind's eye, she replayed scenes from

26

"The Sorcerer's Apprentice" as Mickey struggled to tame the out-of-control celluloid broomsticks.

One sweltering summer night, Aunt Dot and Daddy had taken her to the drive-in movie theater to see Walt Disney's Fantasia. They had watched the film from the tailgate of the farm truck. Zane remembered Daddy teasing her as her feet swung in concert with each animated sequence, speeding up and slowing down with the music. Whereas Mickey had wielded an ax against the multiplying broomsticks, Zane added an oversize claw hammer in the grasp of his gloved hand. She shaded the hammer with the side of her pencil. For her birthday the previous year, Aunt Dot had given Zane a metal tool box and had wrapped each tool, a wrench, a flathead screwdriver, a pair of pliers, and a claw hammer, individually in pages from the funny papers so Zane would have more gifts to unwrap. Despite Aunt Dot's troubles and taciturn nature, Zane appreciated her attempts to make life on the farm bearable.

Zane also recalled Fantasia night, as she thought of it, ending with the three of them going for root beer floats. It was the only time they ever went anywhere together, the three of them, that she could remember. Zane had seen a lady teacher from school at the Dog and Suds but, being too shy, had turned away when she waved.

Most Saturday nights that summer, Zane would go for a ride with Daddy and they would listen to the radio. Crooning together to Hank Williams heart-breaks songs, together they traversed narrow blacktop highways into town. Zane lived those sad country songs first hand at the age of six, as Daddy would leave the radio on as he dropped in on a tavern. He'd say, "I'm gonna drop in and say hello." As Daddy drank beer from a barstool, Zane perched in the cab of the farm truck singing with Hank.

One of the establishments was owned by a nice lady who

often sent out a hamburger for Zane. One time she gave Daddy two Nancy Ann Storybook dolls with instructions he give them to his little girl for Christmas. Daddy knew he wouldn't be in Wisconsin much past harvest, U. S. Steel was hiring again, so he tossed them to her at the end of the night when he returned to the truck.

Zane shaded the wooden slats of the water buckets, bringing out exaggerated wood grain with each stoke. Zane had written to Daddy in Chicago, but she hadn't seen him since late summer. By Halloween, Momma had arrived and taken her by train, first out for breakfast to tell her all about their new life together, and then to St. Joe. Zane had brought the two Storybook dolls with her from the farm to the house on Hawthorne with the steep terrace. They sat on a shelf in her bedroom with a child's pair of Dutch clogs and a set of pewter miniatures that Daddy had brought home from Europe.

Zane looked at the clock across from the reception desk. Nearly an hour had passed since she first sat down. Then she noticed the desk was empty. Taking a deep breath, Zane carefully slid her sketch pad into her satchel so as not to tear the paper on Momma's present, a book, and walked with purpose toward the elevators. She passed under another heavy crucifix hanging on the wall. Her constant fear was discovery by the authorities. School administration learning a fifth-grade girl was staying on her own. Utility companies catching on the bills had not been paid. And now hospital personnel finding someone under the age of 16 on the premises. Thinking better of taking the chance of finding Momma by taking the elevator, she headed for the stairwell.

Zane ascended to the second floor and peeked out into the hall. Hearing nothing but smelling Lysol, Zane started down the hall. Around a corner stood a man with a mop and bucket cleaning the floor. Perhaps recalling Mickey's dilemma, she quickly returned to the stairs and ascended to the next floor.

Zane had just reached the landing of the third floor when the door flew inward. Nowhere to hide, she backed up to the wall behind the door, willing herself invisible. A man on a mission dashed down the steps, turning at the landing. So stunned was she, Zane couldn't speak. Instead she followed in his wake, taking two steps at time to keep up. When he reached the foot of the stairs, he sensed someone following him and turned. "Zane Elizabeth! What are you doing here?"

"The bus stop is this way," Zane said.
"Ah, but we are not taking the bus," Daddy said. "Follow me."

They passed under the gaze of the benign Mary and baby Jesus. "I just didn't want to tell you about your Momma with those Sisters burning holes in me with their eyes."

Zane followed her father a block in the opposite direction of the bus stop to a shiny black two-door hardtop. "Your chariot awaits," Johnnie said, bowing and beckoning her to step in the passenger side.

"Daddy, is this Ford yours, for real?!" Zane asked, incredulous.

"Let's just say Lady Luck smiled on me. And it ain't just any old Ford. This here is a Thunderbird," Johnnie explained. "Let's go for a spin."

Tires spun on the icy street surface, true to his word, as they pulled away from the expired meter.

"You can turn on the radio," Johnnie said. "I just got into town this morning. I haven't had lunch, have you?"

Zane had not only not eaten lunch; her last meal had been a

small can of peaches for dinner the evening before. They drove in silence, save for Gene Autry singing "Up on the Housetop." Within blocks Johnnie parked nose first under the shadow of a smiling giant black cat head with white neon whiskers. Perched at the lunch counter of Katz Drugstore, they ordered Christmas eve dinner. The place was uncharacteristically empty save for the two diners at the counter. Zane ate a tuna melt and Johnnie had a tenderloin sandwich. "You know, there's a lot of places you can't get a tenderloin. They look at you like you're crazy."

As they shared an order of French fried potatoes between them, dipping each fry in a shared puddle of tomato ketchup and salt, Daddy filled her in on Momma's condition.

"She's as yella as that lemon meringue," he said, pointing to a piece of pie in the display case. "Doctors say she has hepatitis. Musta got it in that god-forsaken asylum she went last spring. They fried her brain but good. Wouldn't doubt

33

she got infected there. Either that or from her new man, Bob."

"Mr. Allison doesn't live with us anymore," Zane explained. In so saying, Zane wasn't sure if she was defending Momma or Mr. Allison.

"I know," Daddy said. "Anyway, once they get the jaundice under control, she can come home. I can stay for a few days and then I gotta get back. I just wanted to see my girl for Christmas."

Daddy laid money on the counter and swung her satchel over his back. "Lands, girl, what you got in this here bag, rocks?" he joked.

Zane blushed but knew the satchel wasn't that heavy. "I brought a present for Momma. It's a book," she said, explaining the contents. "And my drawing papers."

"That reminds me!" Daddy said, snapping his fingers. "I gotta little something for you back in the car."

"But you already gave me a gift, my Storybook dolls," Zane reminded him.

"Yeah, but those were really from Toots. I wanted to give you something myself."

Back at the Thunderbird, Johnnie inserted a key on a rabbit foot keychain in the ignition to start the car. Sitting in the close confines of the front seat, Johnnie rubbed his hands together for warmth as Zane waited with anticipation. Johnnie reached behind the seat for a brown paper sack and handed the bag to Zane.

She drew out a tin paint box. The word *Watercolour* was spelled with a "*u*" on the lid. The lower right read "Made in

England." Pictured on the brilliantly colored lid was a busy shipping scene, depicting two children, a boy with a spyglass and a girl painting the scene before them. In the foreground a huge cobalt ship rode above the ocean, the words Royal Blue adorning its prow. Dock workers unloaded cranes onto the ship in the background. Busy workers bustled below with barrel-laden hand carts and pulled on ropes to moor the vessel. The driver of a green flatbed delivery lorry sat behind the steering wheel on the right side of the cab. An orange train engine parked on tracks parallel to the wharf. Zane's finger traced the contrail of a modern jet airplane flying overhead, as a tug disappeared in miniature as it pulled away from the ship. Seagulls gamboled amidst fluffy clouds dotting a cerulean sky.

Enchanted, Zane lifted the tin lid to find nine rows of twelve rectangles of color. She marveled at all the hues of blue, the variations of green, an array of yellows, and the many shades of red. A crisp blue-handled paint brush nestled in a recess in the center of the palette. A shallow mixing tray shone bright white, waiting for red and yellow to paint a sunrise.

Zane didn't know what to say. How could she adequately thank him for such a treasure? Instead she admitted, "I didn't know you were coming. I don't have anything for you."

"Sure you do," Johnnie consoled, pointing to his cheek. "Gimme a sugar."

Zane kissed him on the cheek, first tentatively then threw her arms around his neck and hugged him tight.

That night, secure in the knowledge that Daddy was sleeping in the front room on the couch and with Nosie curled by her side on the bed, Zane fell asleep in the house with the steep terrace on Hawthorne. She dreamed of a dead chicken she had seen at the farm, frozen to the ground. Bringing herself out of the nightmare, she considered praying. For if a chicken died and was gone forever, what happened to people she loved who died?

Zane didn't know any words to begin praying, and thoughts of the days and months since she had last attempted prayer flitted in and out of her mind. She worked up some words but had yet to summon the courage to address the Almighty. She didn't know a word of Scripture, but she had memorized some of the quotes Daddy always said, giving her insight into his beliefs. He said things like, "Gold is where you find it. If you have an opportunity to do something that's wrong but pays well -- do it! You can seek God's forgiveness later with the money in the bank!"

As it was almost Christmas, she counted on God being of a mind to overlook some of their more flagrant violations. She figured it must be around midnight, but she couldn't be sure. She looked out the window at the street light at the bottom of the terrace. She had never believed in Santa Claus, and God frightened her, but she had a good feeling about the Infant Christ whose birth had been heralded by a star, that He had the power to save Momma and protect Daddy. Maybe she could pray to Jesus.

One time she had found a letter from her grandmother, Momma's mother, and it was full of Bible verses. But those words had been used against Momma. Maybe Zane ought not to pray after all. Maybe she shouldn't chance reminding God about Momma, in case he'd forgotten and that was all that was keeping her alive. Prayerless, she fell back to sleep.

"Dozy Doats"

Now & Again

I've been peering into the void. It's not as deep as I feared.

Maybe that's because I now have the advantage of knowing I

came out on the other side. My sight doesn't run purely

chronological so there's no use trying to impose an order.

What I see occurs not as memories but as events happening

all at once. I can understand where you might miss the

segues and loops.

I tried to forget Mother's letters and hadn't read Dad's

journal for years. Turns out we had our own Simon Stimson

right in our midst. He's one of those Grover's Corners

residents. Took his own life. Nature protects the ignorant for

a time. Our Town refers to the real hero of the scene not

being on the stage at all, and "you know who that is." He

says, "It's like what one of those European fellas said: every

child born into the word is nature's attempt to make a perfect

40

human being." I don't have any idea what he's talking about, but I say it's Zane. She's a great grandma many times over now, but I still hear echoes of her childlike prayers. That Stage Manager says there's an act after this one, and I reckon you can guess what it's about. Life imitates art. I'll leave it at that.

March 1955, St. Joseph State Hospital

In the middle of the night, the person in the bed on the other side of the room gasped reflexively. She could not see the insentient body, but the nocturnal noise emitting from behind the curtain caused the woman to stir and reach instinctively for something under the sheet. Closing her fingers around a Bible, she stilled her panicked breathing.

She opened her eyes and peered at the ceiling, willing her brain into action. With her free hand, she traced circles in her

41

scalp to stimulate concentration. Her hair felt different. It needed to be fixed.

An impression flickered. A man, her dad, going to town for glue. For her. For her dolly. Her Dolly's hair. She felt special. He bought glue, just for her, to fix Dolly's hair. Maybe they could glue her hair back. Mother must never know about her hair, that she needed to fix it. Mother didn't think it was necessary to make a special trip to town just to fix Dazy's Dolly's hair. Dazy, that was her name. She was Dazy.

There was another dolly. Two of them. Smaller dolls with curly hair. Storybook dolls. They belonged to the girl in the Bible. Her name was on the slip. The dolls were from her father. Like her own Dad, the girl's daddy had given her dolls.

Once when the girl had been much younger, Dazy had given

42

the girl a doll, too, for Christmas. Zane had been so upset with her because Dazy had sent her to play in her room after dinner for several nights. Zane, that was the girl's name, her daughter. Zane had no way of knowing Dazy was stitching a silky green and yellow mattress and pillow by hand for her new doll. Dazy wanted the doll to be a surprise, but the only way to work on the mattress and pillow in secret in the tiny apartment was to send Zane to her room. The isolation had worked, and Zane was delighted by the doll and her hand sewn silky bedding. Dolly, as she was named, joined Obeob, Okeob, and Mountairy as the girl's friends when they lived in the apartment in Chicago.

When Zane was born, she had been no bigger than Dolly. Once when Zane was just a baby, Dazy had taken her by train to Nebraska to visit Dazy's widowed mother for the very first time. Johnnie was not back yet from the war. Seated next to them on the train was a highly decorated officer in uniform, traveling to be reunited with his family. He told Dazy he

43

would be meeting a grandbaby for the first time at the next

station. His first grandchild and a boy at that. He said he

didn't have much recent experience with babies and hadn't

been around much to help with his own children when they

were tots. "Can I hold her?" he'd asked. He'd bounced baby

Zane and they'd cooed at one another. Doting came so

naturally to him, and the baby took to him right away,

reaching for his shiny medals.

When Zane began to fuss, Dazy had reached to take her back,

but the officer offered instead to give the baby her bottle.

Dazy had been reluctant at first to allow a stranger to feed her

daughter, but as they would be seated together for a few

hours, and he genuinely seemed to want to feed Zane, Dazy

saw no harm. She enjoyed the few minutes of relief his

attention brought and rationalized that she might be helping

him prepare for his role as a granddad. Dazy recalled the

ache of realization that Zane would never be able to call

anyone "Granddad."

When the man on the train burped Zane, she spit up on his uniform. Dazy had dabbed at his ribbons and stripes with a cloth diaper, but the officer had seemed amused at the inconvenience. He had laughed. Said he'd certainly experienced worse matter all over his uniform. That's the way he put it, matter. In fact, he said he'd better get used to baby slobbers and spit. He conceded he was sure glad his daughter-in-law would be the one taking care of the boy's poopy drawers. His son would probably just stick Georgie with a diaper pin with his fumble fingers.

Dazy was startled that she recalled the baby boy's name, Georgie, because it had only been mentioned in passing. Dazy wondered if Georgie's grandfather, or maybe his son, had been named George. In her mind, she thought of the man as being a general or something, but maybe she was confusing him with George Washington. She looked at the Bible she was clutching. She hadn't even opened it, yet she knew her name, her daughter's, her husband's, and the never

met grandchild of a one-time acquaintance. Maybe

remembering the interlude with the officer bode well for all

her memories returning.

Dazy lay in the hospital bed and tried to recall what had

happened next. She and Zane had arrived at their destination.

Mother had sent her regrets with one of Dazy's nephews who

met the train to fetch them. Mother had a headache. Dazy and

Zane were instructed to stay in town with Enid's brother,

Dazy's uncle, and they would all come out to the farm in the

morning at which time Mother would meet her newest

grandchild.

Light from the opaque window panes filtered through the

wire mesh which reinforced them. As daybreak sent shadows

from the room, Dazy noticed dust motes hanging suspended

in the air. Little particles like the ones rising off the mohair

seats of her uncle's car. She could even smell the dust

puffing off the upholstery as she recalled the old Buick they had piled into the next morning to make the 10-minute trip out to the home place where her mother had stayed on after Dad had died.

On the drive to the house, Dazy's uncle retold the story her Dad had told time and again of their moving the house from town to the country. It had taken a team of mules three days to go the distance. It occurred to Dazy that it had taken her and the baby the same amount of time to travel from Chicago to the homestead, but she would have reached the house earlier had they not been compelled to stay the night in town. With equal parts anticipation and dread, Dazy rehearsed her introduction of her baby to her mother. Mother had so many grandchildren that one more wasn't likely to seem all that special.

Dazy had wondered if her mother would put the two of them up in her old bedroom. She had shared the room with a dwindling number of older sisters, who one by one, moved off the farm over the years, leaving Dazy to a room of her own. Had Mother kept it as it was when Dazy had left home at 18, taking little with her besides two hand-me-down traveling outfits in a broken valise? Would the bare walls bear any trace of the images they had once displayed?

In addition to her hand-me-down wardrobe, Dazy had fled with an album stuffed with her sketches. Hollywood film starlets and leading men of the silver screen had covered the walls of the misshapen little room with the angular ceiling and dormers until Mother, in disapproval of all things suggesting sin, made her take them down.

Dazy had spent hours drawing realistic likenesses from movie magazines. She loved shading the eyes, pouting the lips, arching the eyebrows, and filigreeing the hair of Ginger Rodgers, Zasu Pitts, Thelma Todd, Loretta Young, Mary Miner, Alice Faye, and Claire Trevor. Balancing her portfolio were the masculine likenesses of George Arliss, Guy Kibbe, Richard Dix, Jack Oakie, Laurel and Hardy, and Will Rogers. The pantheon of stars labeled by name in precise reproductions of ornate fonts had looked down upon the room.

Dazy had been right. Zane, her precious Zane, had seemed only one more fussy baby to Enid, a grandmother many times over. Enid questioned the name Dazy had given the child and said she much preferred the use of time-tested family names. Her own name, Dazy, although admittedly uncommon in spelling, was a tribute to a great ancestor of Enid's whose parents perhaps were not familiar with the flowery spelling. It was no use trying to explain to her mother that Dazy alone, Johnnie was overseas, had picked Zane because she was reading a Zane Grey novel at the time of her daughter's birth. She liked the sound of Zane and thought the baby girl might need every bit of advantage a strong name might convey. The middle name did have definite family connections,

49

Johnnie's family.

Although her mother was none too impressed with her baby
or her choice of moniker, Dazy liked to hope Dad would
have made over the baby as the man on the train had. Maybe
granddads in general were far less critical. And Dazy had
been right about her room; she found it exactly as she had left
it, patchy baldnesses in the wallpaper from the fallen stars,
the Hollywood types, their removal the only sign of its
previous tenants.

December 27, 1955, Sister's Hospital, St. Joseph, Missouri

Dazy took in the institutional setting she found herself in
now. A crucifix hung on the wall opposite the bed. She
looked in the side table mirror and was relieved to see her
pallor was no longer as jaundiced as it had been. A wrapped
Christmas present lay on the table. Someone had come by
and left a gift. Dazy opened the package to find a book by

Steinbeck. Dazy thought of Zane, at home by herself. She hoped the pup was good company for Zane. Dazy had to get home to them. Had to get back to work. Had to do whatever was necessary to keep the house, so she could keep them all together.

She thought of the wall. The terrace wall. Its collapse under heavy March rains had been the last straw. A retaining wall on the Hawthorne property had washed away with the weight of the spring deluge because it had been improperly constructed. The insurance adjuster had said since the wall was not connected to the residential structure, her homeowner's insurance wouldn't cover the damage, which amounted to thousands of dollars. Without a means of venting, water was unable to drain, and the wall eventually gave way, unleashing the terrace. With no means of allowing release, the pressure proved too much.

Dazy could relate. She had buckled like the wall under the

strain of a second collapsed marriage, Mother's out of context criticism and epistolary barrage, and the constant concern for providing a stable home environment for Zane and even sweet Nosie.

A melody began to play in her head. Woodwinds and brass. No, the music was definitely coming from a distant radio, one tuned to a Big Band station in another room. Barely audible syllables, sense and nonsense, slid down the hall: *Mairzy doats and dozy doats and liddle lamzy divey / A kiddley divey too, wouldn't you?* Dazy strained to hear the song. *Mairzy doats*, yes, Dazy was a farm girl. She had hauled countless buckets of oats to feed the horses. She could relate to the song lyric.

Exhausted from her mind's journey but grateful for the mixed blessing of her intact memories, Dazy fell asleep to the music. In her hand she held a copy of *East of Eden*, the Christmas gift from Zane.

Johnnie Neiglick

Born to German parents who passed through Ellis Island on their way to a greater promise in America, Johann was the third son of Stefan and Elizabeth Kronstein. His mother died in a Chicago tenement fire, but not before seeing to the rescue of her small children. The grief of losing his wife and an inability to speak English proved too overwhelming for Stefan, who abandoned his children and was never heard from again. Years later Johnnie would see to it that his mother's sacrifice for her children was not forgotten when he insisted upon Elizabeth as his newborn daughter's middle name. He let her mother pick the first name so Zane it was.

The Kronstein boys were sent together to an orphanage and from there dispersed into separate foster homes, never to reunite. At least that was the case with the youngest Kronstein. Given the name Johann at birth but re-named Johnnie as a means of assimilation, Stefan and Elizabeth's youngest child had no clear recollection of his brothers' real names.

Thus, at age three, Johnnie was reborn. In the early years, had they tried looking for their younger brother Johann, his brothers might have found him given the derivative nature of his new appellation. Ironically, whereas one naming, that of his daughter, was to remember his first family, Johnnie's own renaming, not his first sobriquet but a subsequent surname change, would cause his brothers to lose contact with him forever. There was no slip of paper in a drawer on which to preserve his identity.

As if following the unscripted playbook for such tragic situations in the early years of the twentieth century, Johnnie met with neglect and abuse at the hands of those charged with his upbringing. Time and again he fled. At an age most children were learning their alphabet, Johnnie was learning how to stay alive. The German spoken in his home had not prepared him for life among the English-speaking masses, so he became a selective mute. At age six, he feigned appendicitis so he could enjoy the luxury of food and a warm bed provided by the superfluous appendage's removal and his subsequent hospitalization.

Johnnie was labeled dumb by social workers who never heard him say a word. Whether his inability to talk began as a charade, was due to a lack of fluency in English, or resulted from physical and emotional abuse is pure speculation, but as a surprisingly garrulous adult, Johnnie claimed not to have spoken a word from the time he was six to age ten when he found favor with a neighborhood kid named Allie, another Kraut who at thirteen had already earned a reputation for running bootleg liquor. Allie's folks, Al Sr. and Irene, took a shine to their son's new pal and thought maybe if Allie had a little brother to look out for, he might not find so much trouble. Providing a haven and a substitute family, the Neiglicks took Johnnie in off the streets, giving him a place to call home, a purpose, and their last name.

Big Al, as Al Sr. was called, made a name for himself at the Chicago Museum of Science and Industry, where he was in charge of the project to restore the captured German submarine, the U-505, for display. Part of Al's motivation for devoting time to the restoration was out of loathing for atrocities perpetrated by those whose Teutonic heritage he shared.

In appreciation for his efforts, the American naval commander responsible for the U-505's capture presented Big Al with a signed copy of his autobiographical *Twenty Million Tons Under the Sea*. Inside the book, Rear Admiral Daniel V. Gallery, USN, wrote the following: *Museum of Science & Industry, October 17, 1956*. To: *Albert Neiglick in appreciation of your work restoring the U505. D.V. Gallery Radm USN.*

Years later, when Johnnie was the only remaining Neiglick, and an adopted one at that, the book became one of his prized possessions until he gave it to his daughter for safekeeping. He moved around too frequently to keep track of material possessions. But as he was in his early twenties and a newly minted man, one with a new last name, Johnnie was afforded the self-confidence to search for a job. He found employment making screws for a small clock company. It was there he met a pretty dark-eyed receptionist, fresh off the farm.

At 18, Dazy Wakefield earned $18 a week. She thought life would be divine if she could continue at that pace, earning a salary equivalent to her years. Dazy rotated between the homes of two married sisters in Chicago but had no place to call her own. Johnnie summoned the courage to ask her for a dinner date to a spot that made the world's best potato pancakes. The whirlwind courtship with Johnnie resulted in a premature consummation followed by a visit to a justice of the peace to legitimize the relationship. The coming of their daughter Zane would have created the tableau of a sweet

little family if Johnnie had not been drafted before her birth.

Dazy worried her husband might meet his death in his

father's homeland, a fate similar to that of a tragic number of

farm boys with whom she had graduated high school. Very

close to her own father who was gravely ill, Dazy's greatest

fear was that her daughter would grow up without one.

Dazy needn't have worried. Instead of on a battlefield,

Private Neiglick found himself on the French Riviera, where

he landed the cushy job of driver for officers on R&R during

the Second World War. Unlike most returning servicemen,

Johnnie was disappointed to be marching home. He was

anxious to meet his daughter, but, perfectly suited for

discretion by his learned ability to keep his mouth shut,

Johnnie had never lived better than when his responsibilities

for Uncle Sam had been limited to escorting officials to

brothels and casinos.

Life back in the States after the war was uneventful by comparison. In her husband's absence, Dazy had continued to work long hours to support herself and their daughter. Upon her husband's return, she adjusted to life as a homemaker, hopeful in the expectation that the small nest egg she had been nursing would make a tidy down payment on a house. Johnnie did not share her vision of the American Dream. A manufacturing job for U.S. Steel saw the family through, but Johnnie never adapted to life as full-time breadwinner, husband, and father. Little in his upbringing had prepared him for those expectations. He sought excitement at racetracks and a livelihood as a card sharp, just not a very good one. Gambling losses wiped out Dazy's savings and then they lost the car. One day she came home to find the living room furniture missing. There was nothing material left to lose. They eventually divorced, Dazy having had her fill of his profligate ways. Johnnie's luck ran out and he found himself working as an occasional factory worker, and even, for a time, as a door-to-door salesman.

It was as an itinerant farm hand that Johnnie visited his

growing daughter one summer on the farm where she was

staying with his ex-wife's sister. He expected to find Zane

living in an idyllic rural setting with a happy family of four.

What he found were the charred remains of a formerly

thriving enterprise. Any hope of hiring on like a returning

prodigal dissipated when he found Zane and her aunt the sole

inhabitants of what was once a lovely farm.

In what was likely the most selfless act of his life, Johnnie

went to work resurrecting the place and bunked in the loft

over the garage. In return for his work, he fell asleep each

weekday night in an old-fashioned sleigh that served as his

bed, one that Zane dreamed of riding in during the

discontented winters of her confinement on the farm. Every

Saturday that summer, he and Zane enjoyed a night on the

town. He would stop off for a drink, leaving the keys to the

farm truck in the ignition so his daughter could tune in to the

Grand Ole Opry.

Mornings her daddy was up at dawn, joining Zane in the kitchen for a breakfast of buckwheat pancakes. The maple syrup came from New Hampshire, provided by a distant relative. The three of them would eat in silence. One morning Johnnie looked at Dot and said, "Tell me about the bullet hole in the refrigerator."

That broke the ice. Dot laughed as she recounted the story of how her son's .22 had discharged in the kitchen when he was cleaning rabbits, striking the Frigidaire. For a time, the sun shone through the gingham curtains, brightening their prospects. It was the age of the automobile, and one evening they crowded into the pickup's cab and headed into town. The three of them took in a picture show at the drive-in theater and went for root beer floats at a drive-in restaurant. The next morning, a Sunday, Dot served the buckwheat pancakes but seemed returned to her former self, the clouds once again blocking the sun. Dot had forgotten how to be happy, and that brief reminder the night before only served to sadden her.

Johnnie left for Chicago later in the week. A buddy said U.S. Steel was hiring and that war veterans were given priority. He said goodbye to Zane and thumbed a ride to the train station so as not to trouble Dot.

June 1950

Shortly before her parents divorced and Zane had gone to live on her aunt's farm for three years, Johnnie took Zane to the park as he often did while Dazy, at age 23, earned $18 a week as a secretary to support their family. Zane begged Daddy to swing her, just one more time. Johnnie had been pushing Zane on the swing, running in circles with her on the

62

merry go round, and catching her at the bottom of the slide at the park all afternoon, but he agreed. "One more time," he consented. "Then we need to go pick up Momma from the office."

It was during that one last time in Chicago that Zane bailed from the swing prematurely, hoping Daddy would catch her. She put out her arm to brace for impact when he didn't. Her first broken bone, at age four, resulted in a heavy plaster L-shaped cast. Daddy and Momma wrote their names on the cast, as did a few of their neighbors. Daddy even signed for Obeob, Okeob, and Mountainary, Zane's invisible playmates, and Dolly, her inanimate one.

The novelty of the cast compensated for the pain of the break, its weight and inconvenience made tolerable by attention and autographs for the span of about a week. Then the cast began to stink. It grew smellier as spring gave way to early summer. Zane had to bathe with care and absolutely

63

could not go swimming, so when Daddy came home and announced they were going to escape the heat of the city by going to the beach, Zane was inconsolable.

The half-day drive from Chicago to Saugatuck, Michigan, in Daddy's new Ford coupe would be an adventure, he promised. They would picnic along the lake shore drive. Momma packed Zane's polka dot romper and some muslin to wrap her cast so Zane would be able to sit in the sand. The mere thought made Zane more miserable.

The Neiglicks stopped for drinks at roadside gasoline stations along the way. As attendants filled the tank, checked the tire air, and washed the windscreen, Johnnie let Zane select a soda pop from the chest cooler. Dazy purchased a pair of sunglasses. "More Bounce to the Ounce," he announced as they carried ice cold Pepsi-Colas to the car. He joked that it was too bad Zane hadn't bounced like the slogan when she'd launched herself from the swing.

At a roadside park, the family spread a blanket and ate ham

salad sandwiches and pickles Dazy had packed. Dazy

brought out a box Brownie Kodak camera. Since Zane

wouldn't be able to play in the water at the beach, Dazy let

her operate the camera. Zane balanced the camera with her

casted arm to photograph her parents: Dazy in shades behind

the wheel of the Ford coupe, Johnnie smiling at Zane as he

leaned back on the driver's side door. Dazy and Johnnie

eating on the blanket. Dazy and Johnnie back to back.

Dazy laughed all over again as she retold the story to Johnnie

of having received a photograph of Zane in the mail. In the

picture, Zane smiled at an unseen street photographer outside

their apartment. Wearing a cowboy outfit and sitting atop a

black and white Shetland pony, Zane modeled oversized

chaps, a bandana, and a rumpled straw hat. Zane, before she

was even school age, had paid the travelling photographer the

two dollars from her piggy bank without her mother's

knowledge. Dazy had been so surprised and delighted to receive the picture in the mail postage paid.

They arrived at Saugatuck just as news hit of the most catastrophic domestic airline disaster of all time. Northwest Orient Airlines Flight 2501 had departed LaGuardia enroute to Minneapolis but had plummeted into Lake Michigan, taking fifty-five passengers and three crew members to their watery grave. Even more alarming than the threat of drifting debris and wreckage were unconfirmed reports of body parts floating ashore. Beaches were closed and no one, not only Zane with her cast, was permitted to swim.

On the return trip, Daddy had wanted to stop by a racetrack for a bit of fun since they hadn't been able to get any closer to the beach than the boardwalk. Dazy and Zane waited in the car while Daddy placed bets on the ponies. Not the ones like Zane had her picture made on, but the ones whose speed held their destiny. Dozing in the sun-warmed car, Zane dreamt of L-shaped casts and sundry body parts washing up on a sandy beach where she sat, wrapped in muslin.

The Enid née Coleman Wakefield Letters

Her husband and youngest daughter may have recorded the events of their daily lives in journals, but Enid née Coleman Wakefield had no time for such self-indulgence. But inspired by the aunt who had written poetry while the Founding Fathers were drafting preambles, Enid had developed her own habit of writing. On their wedding day, each of her children received a special letter. In it, she would remind the children of the responsibilities incumbent upon them due to their lineage. Special emphasis was given to the maternal side of their heritage, with Enid providing at least a page tracing the Coleman name back to New Hampshire and the 1670s. The next paragraph spanned the Atlantic where thankfully their story began in Portsmouth, England, rather than in Ireland as some might think. The Wakefields were from Ireland, but she did not devote much ink to developing that fact.

Enid retained in her possession a copy of her great grandfather's will. In 1810, he bequeathed to his wife, in addition to the house, its furniture and stock, all her own wearing apparel. Enid's generosity of heart must have been passed down as a family trait. To one son and each of two daughters, her ancestor left two dollars apiece. Two older sons were appointed executors and divided the land. Enid was particularly proud that one of her Coleman ancestors had purchased said land directly from Governor Wentworth of New Hampshire, who had been assigned the land by King George III. That ancestor had a daughter who had married a lieutenant in the Revolutionary War, entitling their lineage to all privileges due to Sons and Daughters of the Revolution.

No sooner than the "I dos" were done, and Enid would press

a letter into the palm of the newlywed groom or bride,

beginning with her first born and favorites, down to the

younger Wakefields. In addition to apprising her children of

their rights and privileges, Enid dispensed pages of marital

advice. To the presumed heirs of the Wakefield holdings and

to each of their sisters, the wedding letters over time became

their mother's contribution to the nuptials. It was an

expectation she placed upon herself. All seven children.

Nine letters total. Dazy accounted for more than her share,

with the phrase unequally yoked cropping up in each of her

three, creating an epistolary theme.

Enid had fervently hoped Dazy would marry one of the local

farm boys from a good family, but she had to run off to

Chicago instead. Whereas two of her sisters had married

local and then relocated to the city under the protection of their husbands, Dazy had jumped the gun and hightailed it to the city right after graduation where she had mixed with all types. Her youngest was not entirely to blame though. Older sisters Flora and Myrtle had been charged with sharing chaperone duties. Enid suspected each thought the other had her eye on their independent-minded younger sister.

Enid, who herself had been named for a great-great aunt, took to heart that their shared name meant "purity." Purity was a quality she prized above all others. Anything less was despoiled, such as the marital situation of her youngest daughter. The outcome of those unfortunate circumstances resulted in Dazy's first letter from her mother, which arrived by post rather than hand delivery. The letter's conveyance deviated from those of Dazy's siblings because Enid had not been invited to the wedding.

Not that she would have attended. Johnnie Neiglick was

undeniably an orphan. Dazy had written to her mother that although his birth name had been Kronstein, her married name was Neiglick. Enid informed her that any name ending in *-stein* meant he "may well be a Jew boy," which would be worse than not knowing anything about his parents. Enid was charitable in that she wrote that, orphaned as he was, he could hardly be held responsible for not knowing his heritage. However, Enid suggested that this created the distinct possibility that any offspring might bear the stain of an unholy alliance between her Daughter of the American Revolution and a Hun who was also possibly, and unforgivably, tainted by kike blood.

Still, the damage was done, so Enid's letter sought to make the best of a bad situation through liberal use of her favorite passages from Genesis. She drew inspiration from the Eden accounts of Adam and Eve. Enid made a conscious decision not to include references to the many ways in which original sin blighted the human race and signed the letter simply, *Mother.*

71

By the time Dazy married Bob Allison, not only was she a divorcee, but he had already been married twice. Enid knew of only one former alliance and only because during the single time they had visited as a couple, it was with a young boy in tow. Initially Enid gave Bob the benefit of doubt, hoping he was widowed, but he freely volunteered the information that the child, Bobby or Billy or something, lived with his mother. The man had undeniably comely features and a good English-sounding name. Enid was relieved to learn that at least the child was not a bastard, for Bob seemed the type to charm some girl into giving herself over to him.

Zane happened to be present with her mother, her mother's husband, and his son on that visit, having come directly with them from her Aunt Dot's farm. It was only the third time Zane remembered seeing her grandmother, but, in fact, it was the fourth. Enid had met her granddaughter in infancy. Due to the specialness of this fourth occasion, Enid slipped an extra letter in Zane's suitcase as a bonus. She was under no obligation to do so; the letter tradition was for her sons and daughters. Still Enid wondered if this might be the start of a tradition for the next generation, writing to the grandchildren.

In the letter, Enid expressed the hope that Zane had benefited from the fresh air, hard work, and wholesome environment offered in Wisconsin. Seeing her now as a pre-teen, Enid was frankly disappointed. Zane already had blackheads, which were blemish seeds, and would likely be prone to put on excess pounds. Her oily hair was limp and mousy, showing no evidence of the Coleman red hair.

Enid admonished Dazy in her letter to her daughter to take charge of Zane's complexion, her weight, and possibly see about a permanent wave to do something about the child's hair. Continuing the theme begun in the letter to Zane, Enid

73

speculated in that second nuptial missive that although she had greatly hoped that the arrangement for Zane to spend time with her aunt would have been mutually beneficial, it seemed not to have improved Zane's prospects.

Enid went on to express her desire that the child's three-year stay hadn't been unduly burdensome for Dorothy, whose own sweet daughter had been tragically killed when a doctor had struck Joy with his car. Dazy and Zane were in complete agreement with their matriarch on this point. Joy had been undeniably sweet, and her death had come as a crushing blow to Dorothy. That Zane's absence as she went to live with her aunt had left Dazy bereft of her daughter's companionship and her daughter motherless for three years simply did not occur to Enid. She concluded her letter to her remarried youngest daughter with selected passages from the Old Testament's second book, Exodus, making a special effort not to explicitly cite the Sixth Commandment, but leaving room for the Lord to convict Dazy in due course.

74

Enid could never have known she had not been made privy to

certain salient details surrounding Zane's life on the farm

with her aunt. Dazy's sister Dorothy never shared

information with anyone, not those in her household and

certainly not with her mother. During Zane's three-year

sojourn with her sister, Dazy had no way of knowing of the

dissolution of Dorothy's family because she had agreed to

keep her distance. And if Zane didn't crack under

interrogation by school authorities, she was not about to open

up to her distant and disapproving grandmother. Secure in

her ignorance of son-in-law Hal's adultery, their impending

divorce, and her grandson's desertion, Enid planned to write

a cheery hello to Dorothy, as well, offering to come for a

visit in the coming weeks. She would be traveling that

direction to attend the upcoming WCTU spring convention,

as well as take in a W Tri-K rally.

(Throughout their marriage, Theo tolerated his wife's involvement in ladies' leagues and quilting bees as the feminine equivalent of his participation in sporting and hunting events. That she invited each of the girls in turn to attend some of these meetings seemed to him no different from his taking the boys on wolf hunts or to watch high school football games. All the men of his acquaintance served together on various civic, school, and church boards, so it seemed par for the course that his wife and her lady friends would likewise congregate around activities that were of interest to the fairer sex. Until he died in the 1940s, Theo did little to discourage Enid's pride in her heritage and her activism on behalf of temperance. A busy farmer, he loved America, too, and therefore found no fault with the passionate patriotism that was capturing Enid's imagination. The difference between Theo's and Enid's love of country was in its manifestation. Theo was a proud patriot who loved the red, white and blue. Enid's virulent nationalism took the form of hatred. Before the words *xenophobia* and *racism* were in common currency, Enid was circulating their sentiment. Theo even humored Mrs. Wakefield by not complaining when she went off on "convention holidays," as he referred to her Women's Christian Temperance Union weekends. His journal referred to a WCTU convention as "Mama's Blowout." He teased that WCTU stood for "Women Crusaders Taking Umbrance." To a lesser degree was he aware of the encroaching association between those rallies and the ones that sounded so innocuous as to be a radio station's call letters. Theo died not completely aware that the ladies' organization his wife cryptically called "the W Tri-K" was a ladies' auxiliary of the Ku Klux Klan.)

Enid wrote one more letter to Dazy years later. By the time Dazy married her third husband, Lew, her mother had mellowed considerably. Enid had nothing bad to say about this husband. Other than perhaps she questioned his judgment in choosing for his wife, Dazy, a divorcee, as he did, Lew seemed like a gem. Enid prayed that Dazy's previous failed marriage had been so brief that Lew need never know the full extent of the damaged goods he was taking on. "It is best to leave some things unsaid," she said, trying not to be so pointed as to actually spell out that second fiasco of a marriage and certainly not its shocking aftermath. Enid simply provided Leviticus 21:14 as an enigmatic closing. Once home, Dazy looked up the scriptural inspiration for this third letter from the third book in the Old Testament. "He must not marry a widow, a divorced woman, or a woman defiled by prostitution, but only a virgin from his own people."

Enid circa 1965

Though as expected, she wrote singularly to each of her children on the occasions of their marriage, near the end of her life, Enid Coleman Wakefield wrote unexpectedly to her collective offspring and had it copied for distribution. It was the last letter she would ever write. Dated March 5, 1965, the letter arrived shortly before her death, nearly 20 years after Theo had passed, and five years after their daughter Dorothy, their beloved Dot, had died of cancer. The copied letter was evidence their mother's mind dwelled much on regret. In spidery script Enid wrote:

"Dear Children,

You will be surprised to get this letter, but I thought some of you might not know how very sick your father had been. This sickness weakened him, which led to his death too soon. Theo had the typhoid fever for 6 weeks. He lay on the bed with only a sheet over him and the doctor stopped every day to take his temp. Mr. and Mrs. Stanley Hopewell who lived a mile further also had the fever. Dr. Briggs brought little cubes of beef juice and that was all he could have to eat. I had to dissolve one in warm water and feed it to him with a spoon. He lay there for six long weeks and when he did stand up he could hardly walk alone and had a full beard from ear to ear.

He had to go into town to have his beard clipped off and shaved as he had not shaved in all that time. Any time he ate more than the bovine soup, his fever went right back up. I had to sponge off his body 5 or 6 times a day to keep the fever down.

I remember one time Dorothy had a big fall from the cellar door down into the cellar way. And she struck her head on a rock that was in the cellar way. I really spanked her and was always so sorry I did for she did not mean to do that.

It was an accident.

But I was such a poor mother.

Dorothy was so good to go to bed that night without a light of any kind."

The letter went on for several more pages. By this time, Theo had been dead for over 20 years and their daughter Dorothy had been gone five years, reunited in death with her own daughter, Joy. It was evident Dorothy's death prompted lamentation on Enid's part. There was no mention of regret regarding her treatment of Dazy, who in self-deprecation echoed her own mother's words that she was "the only bad child Enid Wakefield ever had." Instead Enid spoke of random remembrances of things past, including the time they moved their house 10 miles. She commented on someone's blooming gloxinias and African violets, programs on the radio, and a flashlight she had purchased. Enid signed the letter, "Mother." As an addendum, she wrote, "This poem is the way I think of my dear husband, Theo Reuben Wakefield." No poem was attached.

The Theo Wakefield Journal

Except for during the bout of typhoid fever that nearly killed Dazy's dad, Theo Reuben Wakefield wrote a short account of the day's events after supper every evening of his adult life.

This practice of journaling was one Dazy, his fourth daughter, would emulate throughout much of her own life. On the day his youngest was born, he recorded the announcement with his usual brevity: *"January 30, Friday: Baby girl, D-, born. Went over to Pa Coleman's and phoned Dr. N-."* Theo knew who baby girl D- was and saw no reason to spell it out. The assembly of letters in Dazy's name would not have struck him as unusual in any way. Like her siblings, the child was named for one of Enid's, his wife's, early relatives, and besides, the one-room school he had attended for three years had not spent much time on the proper spelling of flowers. Thus, D- denoted Dazy in Theo's lexicon and referred to the final child to be born to the Wakefields.

Although Theo and Enid were to have no additional offspring and thus no labor and delivery urgency prompting a telephone call to the doctor in the middle of the night, years later the Wakefields would put in their own telephone line following little Dazy's birth. For the next thirty odd years,

82

Theo would include in the written record of the day's events, any time they would go to town and pay the rent on the phone.

The ledgers were for his own edification, used to record prices of goods bought ("32 cents worth of candy for Christmas") and sold ("three mules, Ned, Jim, and Stub, $75") and as a means of keeping track of meteorological data, rainfall, snow, temperatures. Theo kept meticulous track of the weight of his livestock and of their names. Every mule that ever drew a plow or pig that provided bacon had a pet name. Even the offspring of the Wakefield menagerie had names. One Saturday the 9th, Theo wrote, "Born: Bess's calf, Blossom." Babe's colt, a dapple named Gray, was born in April of 1917. Unlike his offspring, the animals' names were spelled out.

Using Theo's entries, a person could calculate the changing rate of inflation by tracking the prices of shoes for Theo's seven children as they grew. The children, Franklin, Will, Myrtle, Flora, Suzanna, Dot and Dazy, were known respectively as F-, W-, M-, F-, S-, D., and D in his journal. Collectively Theo referred to his offspring as "the kiddies" no fewer than seven hundred and twelve times from the years recording 1903 until his death in the '40s, when they were all grown and had kiddies of their own. His use of initials and quaint terminology might have been considered endearing except for the existence in those days of county KKK auxiliary chapters for women and children, which had names such as Ku Klux Kiddies.

Naturally Theo's kiddies referred to his Wakefield clan (with lower case c-) and to fewer actual family members in the early years. Because daughters Dorothy and Dazy had D names, Theo adopted a period after Dot's name when Dazy came along. A dot for Dot system, if you will. Though the 500-plus page hardbound journal, posthumously and privately published, preserved every journalistic quirk, every misspelling, every capitalization mistake, and every grammatical error, the picture of an intelligent, hard-working, civic-minded, doting father, and God-fearing man is clear. Still, it is hard for the 21st century reader to overlook occasional and casual references to the K.K.K. as if it were the Rotary or American Legion. Theo never mentioned his own involvement in the regional chapters which ranged much further north of the Mason-Dixon line than most ever realized. Still startling acronyms crop up in the record in Theo Reuben Wakefield's own hand, his self- incriminating use of K.K.K seemingly no different from his use of initials for family members.

If Theo included a person's full name, the entry likely related to his in-laws, the Colemans, but often, he stuck to initials. The proud father may have been feeling quite expansive when, on the day of D-'s birth, Theo wrote out "Pa Coleman" rather than Pa C, his usual means of distinguishing between his father-in-law and his own father, whom he referred to simply as Pa.

Entries surrounding the birth announcement of his seventh and final child were typical of his records, including a few weeks later, on Wednesday, February 20: "A genuine blizzard all day, but not cold. 28 degrees. Had a big time catching chickens. Mrs. Wakefield got out and enjoyed some of it." This last was notable not as much for the blizzard, but as for his wife's enjoyment of it. Enid nee Coleman Wakefield, renowned for the long auburn coils pinned tightly atop her head, was not so easily pleased. Within days, the weather turned, Theo reported, meriting all caps. "Monday, February 25: ROADS IMPASSABLE. SNOW DRIFTS EVERYWHERE. Gave cattle load of hay." Few mentions of Mrs. Wakefield enjoying anything again were recorded.

Theo's wife's family, the Colemans, could trace their roots to Colonial America, giving Enid and the Coleman dynasty entre into the exclusive ranks of the Sons and Daughters of the American Revolution. Being DAR was a matter of great pride for the Coleman people. Readers of Theo's journal might detect the subtle humor with which Theo treated any pretentiousness. He respected pedigree in animals, though, because they were incapable of sentience, and therefore unable to give off airs over being the son or granddaughter of so and so.

Theo's other six children, many of whom were teenagers when little D-came along, were expected to work alongside their father on the farm. Shoulder to shoulder with their father and brothers, the sisters plowed, hauled, husked, hayed, mowed, mucked, butchered, fed, planted, slopped, and dragged. In the early twentieth century, farming required a varied vocabulary of verbs to record day-to-day life. Participles aside, snowing, blowing, raining, showering, sleeting, blizzarding, or sizzling, work waited for no man, and not even a child, a girl child at that, was exempt. Any exemption from farm work was the necessary care of an infant or toddler sibling. As only two boys were born to Theo and Enid, it fell to their four daughters to carry on the farm labors when their elder brothers matriculated.

Dazy's family: The Wakefields
Nebraska, early 20th century

Enid was too busy with matters related to preserving her ancestry and with crusading on the evils of drink to dote much on her progeny. And what a hungry hoard they were. Every fruit and vegetable, root or otherwise, the family of nine consumed had to be planted, grown, harvested and prepared. If the bounty allowed, any excess was preserved by means of curing or canning. Meat needed slaughtering. A note in Theo's journal read thusly: "We made sausage and rendered lard. A fine day."

Theo was not the only writer in the family. When she wasn't

in her sitting room studying Coleman genealogy, Enid might be reading the Pentateuch. For one so suspicious of the Hebrew tribe, Enid was devoted to the study of their Levitical texts. She frequently penned unsolicited advice to far flung family members and drafted editorials in opposition to demon alcohol. A charter member not only of the county chapter of the DAR but also a founder of the local league of the Women's Christian Temperance Union, Enid was widely recognized as one in full possession of facts promoting prohibition. Her sober disposition made her the perfect advocate for enacting the 18th Amendment. As she distrusted any politician whose ancestral roots ran less deep than her family's 250 years just because he wore pants, she also voiced support for the 19th allowing women the vote. One of the saddest days of her life was when the 21st Amendment repealed Prohibition.

Enid wrote in the sitting room, but her headquarters were in the kitchen. Nobody, not even any of the four female members of the family, was welcome in her kitchen. And that was just fine with the girls, who, even if not much in evidence from the sparse details of his journal, much preferred the company of their father. They were expected, however, to keep house at day break and day's end, before or after all the outside chores and farm labors were tended to. Enid would deign to criticize the efficacy of their house cleaning but never dropped a quill or a rolling pin to free up an ink stained or flour-dusted hand to help.

But life in the Wakefield home was not all work and no play. Theo courted his wife throughout their married life. She performed her conjugal duties and bore him eight offspring, one of whom died at birth. At one week's end, Theo wrote that he "chored, shaved, took a bath, and etc." On that particular Saturday, the 14th of February, Theo recorded that after finishing drilling oats, "we went to town to the Operetta, Ma and I."

A big raw-boned man, Theo Wakefield was first a Methodist but foremost a family man. Despite having only a third-grade formal education, Theo took part in nearly every aspect of each of his children's schooling. He not only served on the school board, he built, repaired, and provided loads of coal for the school house. Theo wrote that the entire family moved, house and all, noting "the house arrived in the p.m." While he was getting lumber to replace the front porch on their relocated house, he purchased enough to replace the school outhouse pit and floor. He negotiated to hire a Miss Katie Burns to teach for $80 for the entire year in 1921, but in another year Miss Lucille Lonergan must have driven a hard bargain, as her contract was for $45 a month.

Any holiday that came and went did so with a notation about the day's happenings. Theo recorded that they got but one pocket gopher between them on one New Year's Day outing with the lads. As he also noted it blew up cold, it can be assumed they might have got more gophers had the weather been more conducive to getting gophers. One snowy

Thanksgiving, son F- played football in a foot of snow in a

nearby town, with Theo noting they had to take a V-plow to

mark the boundary lines. "F- said the ball was slipry [sic]as a

watermelon seed," it was so hard to keep hold. Christmas

preparations merited more detail, one instance recording an

account of plowing through 17 inches of snow to deliver two

dressed turkeys for delivery by train to Wakefield relatives

living in Chicago.

Any time the Wakefields went to town, an entry included the

trip's purpose, be it paying taxes, paying bills, paying rent, or

paying on bank notes. Amounts were dutifully noted and

never exceeded three digits. In one entry, Theo all but

shouted: "ALL THAT WE HAVE IS OURS. WE OWE NO

MAN A CENT!!"

Theo made particular note of Election Days on any Tuesday

set aside for civic participation, even working on the Election

Board and collecting signatures in favor of or opposition to whatever measures might be on the ballot. Of the results of the 1932 Presidential Elections, Theo wrote "DEMOCRATS SWEEP," adding that he, along with F- and W-, went to a neighbor's house to listen to the election results on the radio, not having one of their own. A Hoover man himself, he named a white calf born to Sweetpea, *Herby Hoover*. Theo distrusted the policies of the incoming administration and feared their policies would be the ruination of the whole dern country.

Accounts of afflictions abound in Theo's diary, ranging from intestinal grippe, lock-jaw, and typhus, to pneumonia, whooping cough, colic, and bloat. He writes of once having mistaken soap for more curative minerals. "I took a dose of washing powder. About ate my insides out. Mighty sick and bloated."

Theo's journal chronicles the transition of transportation by horseback and mule-drawn buggies to the earliest automobiles. His first up-close encounter read, "Mr. and Mrs. Geo. H. Coleman and Mr. and Mrs. Abner Duncan drove up in a Velie Auto-mobile." By 1916, Theo writes, "Pet's mule was born. I plowed on Dad's in a.m. I harrowed in p.m. and went to town with (someone named) T M and BOUGHT A FORD CAR (Model T), $466.60 plus $3.05 for a license, $469.65. (The underlining Theo's for emphasis.) W- harrowed while I was gone. Rained about 2 ins. In eve. T M stayed the night." Living on miles of dirt road, Theo tells of a time he "washed car with Bonami and went to see fizzle of a Carnival." Brand loyalty did not concern Theo, as later he says he bought "a New Shiverelett." That night they "drove the Shivy to town." At least one account in every recorded month said they "dragged the road," a reference to the unpaved dirt lanes connecting them to the outside world.

Many an accident wreaked havoc with their well-being in those days, killing loved ones, some by trains and some by

automobiles. One quite serious mishap involved daughter
Dazy's injury resulting from a horse accident. On one
occasion the girls (plural) fell from the cherry tree, and on
another Theo and Enid arrived home to find W- had
accidentally shot F- in the leg. All such incidents merited the
one mention only, so presumably the subjects mended or
were never hurt that badly to begin with.

Death was an ever-present part of life. Theo marked the death
of his wife's mother by stating "Mother Coleman died at 3:45
a.m." On the same day he goes on to say they went to town
for a plow tongue. That evening all the kiddies went to a
recital. Of his own mother's demise, he waxed more poetic,
"Mother passed out of this life. Mr. M came out to take care
of Mother's body and two men brought the casket out."

The full details surrounding some of the recorded deaths
were omitted for propriety, but Theo and Enid did attend the
funeral of a nephew, a teacher who took his own life. The

latter fact was added as a notation by future generations transcribing their grandfather's journal. Apparently, the young man was distraught over his students' difficulty grasping the knowledge he tried so nobly to impart.

Although not an athlete in any organized sense of the word due to his limited formal education, Theo loved following his sons as they participated in sports. Scores of scores of high school football games are dutifully noted, including one tongue and cheek reference to a game they "barely won, the outcome being 36 to 0." The Wakefield boys played basketball, as well, and one big night played in what he called a "double basketball game." Once they were of a driving age, the boys "took the car to attend the Co. track m-e-e-t." Although the family attended many such county and regional sporting events, they followed national ones by radio. On October 9, 1931, Theo wrote, "We most of us went to town to shop and list in on the World Series of Base ball."

Hunting was not so much a matter of recreation, as one of preservation. Pigeons, fish, and small game were the aim. On a number of occasions, Theo writes of going with other men "on the wolf hunt."

The oldest son and football star, F-, is recorded to have "quit school" before graduation. For days after, Theo recorded all the extra work F- did around the farm. Then F- started courting a gal. Her father, a preacher, married the two and there are numerous references to their coming to the homeplace with kiddies of their own, eventually an even dozen. They often stayed to supper. To supplement his work on the farm, F- turned to selling life insurance policies. Phrases like "double indemnity," "total disability," and "transfer of beneficiary" became part of Theo's lexicon as he undoubtedly overheard his son's pitch to neighbors. F- eventually enrolled in night school and received his diploma about the time the first of his dozen children graduated.

Fifty-two Sundays of every year for nearly half a century, Theo recorded which of his family members went to church. Illnesses of any who did not attend S.S. (Sunday School) or morning and evening services were duly noted. The Sabbath generally included a carry-in dinner on the church grounds or at the home of one of the patriarchs, Pa C or Pa. One quite typical Sunday read, "A fine day. Bobsled, sleigh riding, a cow with a sore tongue, and a chicken pie Church supper." Easter Sundays were different only in that special outfits were purchased for the occasion. Theo notes that on one such Sunday, "two Skinner children was converted."

One winter their church building burned, and the Methodists met with their German Congregational brethren for a time. When the newly erected replacement building was dedicated, Theo writes of the "altar being full all the way around for baptizing." Once the whole family attended a "Holyness Camp Meeting." He noted that W- became a Christian that day. In an uncharacteristic display of emotion, Theo wrote

"BEST DAY EVER" to describe two of his daughters, M- and S-, accepting Jesus.

Although no one could doubt Theo's sincerity or depth of belief, his devotion to ecclesiastical concerns paled in comparison to the fervor of his wife on social and political matters. Her views on theology were also decidedly darker. Though he never touched alcohol, faithfully observed the Sabbath, and did not allow playing cards in his home, Mrs. Wakefield found the faith of her children's father too liberal for her liking. She crusaded as a member of the Women's Christian Temperance Union, organizing showings of anti-saloon films, attending "booze trials," and frequenting meetings in "Kenzington". Enid's DAR heritage and teetotal passion fueled her intolerance for people whose pedigree or viewpoints differed. Theo often remarked with humor that Enid would attempt to prevail upon one or more of her young daughters to attend the junior version of whatever sisterhood meeting she was attending and would be all in a huff if rebuffed.

After 30 years of marriage, Theo and Enid observed their anniversary with a party, serving 12 gallons of ice cream and 14 cakes to over 120 well-wishers. In the aftermath, everyone "got powerful busy" returning all the ice cream freezers to their rightful homes before the couple embarked on a two-week train trip to see the Niagara Falls. They left their only remaining child in the home, 10-year old D-, by herself for the duration. Theo records having stayed in a motel, which cost them "75 cents a head."

In three decades of marriage, there was never any mention of disharmony between the two until one day, Theo noted, he and Enid "Got into a real fuss." On this day, he writes, he came in from unloading a manure spreader to find a "KKK man" in their sitting room.

Dazy's family, Zane and Nosie, and the House on Hawthorne
St. Joseph, mid-20th century

On January third, a week after Zane had chased him down
the hospital steps, Johnnie left for Chicago and a new job. He
had stayed longer than he'd intended, but his daughter had
needed him. In the days following Christmas and in the
second-most selfless acts of his life, Johnnie spent some of
his winnings to catch up on the bills and make the house
payment, hoping to tide them over until Dazy could get on
her feet. The doctor assured him that Dazy would be
discharged as soon as her hepatitis was manageable.

As the house on Hawthorne with the terrace was only four
blocks from school, Zane generally walked. Other
neighborhood kids rode their bicycles to school, weather
permitting. On her first day back, following Christmas
vacation and on his way out of town, however, Johnnie
dropped Zane off at Mark Twain Elementary. Not only was it

blue black cold, Johnnie knew how to make an impression, and he said squiring his daughter to school in a shiny new Thunderbird was bound to make one.

The crossing guards were all sixth graders, and Zane, being in fifth grade, blushed as her dad pulled up to the school. Johnnie handed Zane her sack lunch and her red plaid satchel as if he did this every day. He reached into his pocket and gave her all his pocket change, along with some crumpled bills.

"It's not much," Johnnie said, "but I want you to have a little walking around money." Zane took the money and without counting it, mentally calculated how much she still needed for the bicycle with the basket at the Western Auto. The bike was red and grey and cost $56. She opened the heavy car door and started to step out.

"Oh, I almost forgot!" Zane opened her satchel and pulled

102

out piece of newspaper folded into an oversized envelope tied with a piece of twine. "Now I don't want you to open it 'til you get home, promise?"

"Does this have anything to do with all the secrecy-- you going into your room early last night?" Johnnie teased.

"Just write me when you get home, okay?" Zane said, planting a kiss on her dad's cheek as she stepped out of the car.

"Sweeter than sugar," Daddy said.

Zane was glad the picture had been dry enough by morning for her to wrap it. Inside her father would find a water color of a busy shipping scene. In it a girl with a red satchel stands at an easel painting the scene before her, a black and brown spaniel seated at her feet. A huge cobalt ship rides high above the ocean. The silhouette of a driver at the wheel of a shiny black Thunderbird looks through the open window from the American driver's side. Seagulls gambol in a cerulean sky. In the lower right, the words "Made in U.S.A" are painted in serif.

Once in the classroom, Zane and her classmates hung their wraps on the peg at the back of the classroom. The teacher, Mrs. Silcott, asked Zane about her holiday and inquired after her mother. "She's great. We had a real good Christmas," Zane answered hastily, pretending to look into the deep recesses of her satchel for something. Zane loved Mrs. Silcott and wanted to spare her teacher the embarrassment of knowing anything was amiss.

At lunch, the principal approached the fifth-grade lunch table on stealthy orthopedic shoes. Miss Homerline Coffman had served as principal since the Depression. Generations of students had walked single file one arm's length from either wall along straight tile rows under Miss Coffman's gaze.

"Miss Neiglick, might I have a word with you?" Miss Coffman barked, her sentence an imperative in the guise of a question.

Zane rose from the table, folded the wax paper holding her sandwich and put it back into the lunch sack for the next day's use, and followed Miss Coffman into the hall. Zane stood with her eyes on her Mary Janes and waited for Miss Coffman to speak. She couldn't have been more surprised when Miss Coffman asked, "Is everything okay at home, honey?" Zane shifted her gaze to the brown crepe-soled shoes opposite and followed them up to the man-tailored suit and unfamiliar kindly expression. Speechless, Zane wondered if this might be a trick question. "I happened to note an unfamiliar automobile dropped you off, and Mrs. Silcott reported that a man brought you to school this morning," Miss Coffman explained.

Dazy searched for her answer, one that would safely satisfy

the line of inquiry. "Oh, that was just my Daddy. He has a brand-new car and was going out of town on a business trip. He brought me to school since it was kind of cold." She had no idea if the powers that be at Mark Twain Elementary had access to the usual census of their household. If asked, she would say there were three of them, and no one need be the wiser that for the most part, the third was canine.

Miss Coffman seemed placated by the news that Mr. Neiglick had been the one to bring his daughter, usually a walker, to school. "Well, it's a swell car," Miss Coffman conceded most uncharacteristically.

Walking back to class an arm's length from the cinder block walls lining the hallway, Zane thought how Daddy was right; he knew how to make an impression. This was the second time his presence had been called into question, the third time she had had to answer for him before a school authority.

Back to her normal routine of walking the four blocks home from school, Zane was surprised when Nosie did not meet her at the end of Hawthorne. Nosie's six-day a week routine was to accompany the mailman, Lorenzo Robards, for half of his route. Like Lorenzo, Nosie pledged neither snow nor rain nor heat nor gloom of night would stay the couriers from the swift completion of their appointed rounds, or at least until lunch. Sniffing each day's new smells, Nosie would escort him as far as Lorenzo's home for his noon dinner break, whereupon he would give her water and a biscuit.

Rather than wait for him to eat, Nosie would retrace their steps and smells, moseying her way back to the corner where she would time her arrival to meet Zane at the end of the school day. Zane marveled that her dog's precise internal clock kept such regular time. That she was nowhere to be seen after school alarmed Zane. She walked the rest of the block home unattended and started up the steep steps of the front terrace to the porch, calling for her dog. Maybe Nosie's sense of timing was off since they had been on holiday break. Daddy had taken her to school that morning, so perhaps Nosie had no idea they were back on schedule.

Zane collected the mail left by Lorenzo earlier in the day from the letter box mounted to the house. Relieved not to see overdue bills but dismayed to see her Grandmother's spidery scrawl on the single envelope in the day's post, Zane shifted her satchel on her shoulder and picked up the newspaper. The paperboy Donny Ray had succeeded his older brother Ronny in delivering the evening news. She needed to remember to save some of the change Daddy had given her to pay Donny, who came by every two weeks to collect.

Tucking the Gazette under her arm, Zane bent to retrieve the milk. Their Meadow Gold milkman had left a quart bottle in the insulated metal box on the porch. On cold days the milk turned to icy shards by the time Zane took it inside, the box acting as a thermos to keep the cold out rather than in. She balanced everything to open the unlocked door. They had a key somewhere, but the house remained unlocked at all times, except lately at night when Zane had begun throwing the dead bolt in her mother's absence. Still she worried more that her barring the door would somehow create an obstacle in an emergency than she did about the possibility of an intrusion. So, most of the time the door remained unlocked.

Once inside, Zane set everything down and, finding no sign of the dog in the house, tentatively lifted the receiver of the telephone. Relieved no one on the party line was talking, Zane's fingers dialed Speed and Nadine's number by number, ADams3-3676, her muscle memory taking control. Speed picked up right away. "Speed's Pub," he answered as he always did. Zane ignored his jest and blurted, "Have you seen Nosie?" Speed answered, "Zane, that you? Lemme ask Nadine." Zane could hear him yell, "Nadine!" as the heavy rotary earpiece was laid on the wooden telephone bench.

Nadine came on the line. "Honey, we haven't seen Nosie since she and Enzo came by earlier. Is she missing? Did Johnnie get off okay? We made some special juice if you want to come over and get some to have on hand when your momma gets home." Not knowing which of the inquiries and invitation to address first, Zane choked back a sob. She regained her composure long enough to say, "I'll phone you later, Nadine" and hung up.

It was then she saw Nosie through the kitchen window lying on the patio, a dark silhouette against the light snow. "Please God, please God," she uttered aloud. Steeling herself for whatever the fates had in store, she opened the back door. The dog lifted her head. In immediate relief, Zane rushed to Nosie's side. She petted the dog and checked her all over. There was no sign of injury. Nosie feebly licked the hands that examined her without raising her head. Zane didn't know if please God constituted a prayer, but it had been answered all the same.

Then Zane realized she smelled something like grape jelly. There was a definite aroma rising off the dog. In fact, the whole backyard smelled of Concord grapes in the crisp late afternoon air. Zane rose and looked around, following the strengthening smell. Zane remembered Speed and Nadine's special juice and realized the dog was drunk. Nosie had gotten into the grape mash they used to distill the homemade hooch which had been dumped behind their house.

What's more, it wasn't the first time a dog in Zane's acquaintance and Nosie's lineage had gone on a bender. That's how she knew the dog was hungover and not dying. Although Nosie's father Oscar, a Heinz 57, lapped only water, Nosie's jet black mother Inky had been known to imbibe. One day months earlier Zane and Dazy had visited Dazy's then sister-in-law Carol, Bob Allison's sister. Carol, a dog breeder expecting a third child herself, had stood in the disarray of her partially remodeled kitchen, cigarette in one

111

hand and an empty beer can in the other, lamenting, "What kind of mother am I if I can't even keep my dog sober?" Hours earlier Inky had tipped Carol's beer and had licked up the puddle of Pabst and was out cold on the kitchen floor.

Zane carried her impaired pooch into the house and laid her on the sofa to sleep off her inebriation. Zane started a load of laundry and went into the kitchen for a bowl of water for Nosie. Before she could return she heard a woman's laughter and a voice over the noise of the running water, "I thought we agreed not to let the dog on the davenport."

Zane dropped the bowl in the sink and dashed into the living room. There stood her mother, thin and pale, but smiling. Dazy thanked the taxi driver who had helped her up the steep terrace steps to the door and handed him some bills and coins from a pile on the coffee table next to an unopened letter from her mother, Enid.

Although Zane feared she might hurt her mother if she were

not careful, Dazy crushed Zane with all her strength. Rather than let go of her daughter, Dazy let go of the Steinbeck novel, the one paralleling a family's exile to that of Eden's outcasts. Zane had sent it to the hospital with her father as Dazy's Christmas gift.

"Liddle Lamzy Divey"

Now & Then

Seeing everything at once as I now can, I hardly recognize myself. I imagine it's that way for anyone who undergoes a drastic change in a short amount of time. In my case having nearly expired a couple of times before I died in the earthly sense, I almost looked forward to the time they marked me a goner for good. The first near death was from the humiliation of a failed marriage. If I'd have known then things would only get worse, I'd have seen those as the good ole days. But shouldering blame and shame was nothing compared to seeing Zane somehow marginalized due to our failings,

Johnnie's and mine.

I never expected to be gored by a polled devil who wed me before he was done being married to his second wife. That lily-livered Lothario took me for a fool. He was on to another before he quit me, leaving me with a mortgage and a nervous breakdown. Shocking how that all turned out. Numerous times in fact. Re-Volting, you might even say. But I wrote our names down, remembered who we were, and survived somehow.

It wasn't any green-eyed monster but the bile emesis he infected me with that gave me such a jaundiced outlook and nearly did me in next. Adding insult to injury to irritation, letters from Mother heaped coals upon the ashes I'd made of my life. I always wanted to be cremated but preferred it post mortem. Come to think of it, I'm not rightly sure what they did with my body once I was done with it . . .

Anyway, somewhere in the late 1950s, life started to look up. I found a new job. It meant taking a bus across town each day, but Zane and that silly little spaniel gave me the will to go on. When my knight rode up in a yellow and black shining '57 Chevy and tossed me a lifeline, he pulled me up from the bottom of a broken terrace, I thought I might actually live. Still, I have to go back before I can move forward. Turns out there was so much about Lew I never realized. Things he never said. Not that he was deliberately hiding anything, but he was a modest man who preferred not to remember. Plus, it was in his nature not to bring up painful subjects. I always thought he was trying to protect me, but now I see he was insulating himself against heartache too. Odd how only now do I know about the one who came before me, and incredibly enough after me. More about that later. It was no secret Lew kept a safe deposit box, but I figured it contained family deeds and such. He never spoke much of his time in the Army, so I had no reason to suspect he had held on to mementos of his time overseas--medals, newspaper clippings, military paperwork and commendations. The written pages were a complete surprise. I don't know if they were intended as part of a letter to someone, maybe someone in his family, or her, or if they served as a record tracing the progress of his battalion's advancement behind enemy lines. He saved people and never told me. That was so Lew. Zane would argue the semantics but not the sentiment; Lew was our Savior.

Lew Palmer 1944-45

Lew reread and folded the letter from Janine before putting it back in his uniform pocket. Of all the pain and discomfort this war had meted out, the unscented letter's contents wounded him more deeply. He understood her situation, but comprehension didn't make her decision any less painful. After all, he had told her she might not want to wait for him, that although he intended to return, he couldn't make any guarantee. In his heart though, he was an optimist. He intended to make it back, and he had doubted there would be many others for her to choose from in a time of war, able-bodied anyway. He had been so certain they were destined to be together.

From his cramped position within Old Ironsides 63, a tank belonging to the first armored division and his mobile home away from home with the 777 Tank Battalion, Lew regretted, not for the first time, his decision to enlist. He needed a cigarette. When the armored vehicle came to a stop and the hatch was opened, Lew climbed out with the crew for a smoke.

Surrounded by G.I. jokes and laughter, Lew's mind was elsewhere. One-handed, he flipped open the Zippo and held the lighter to the unfiltered cigarette. Sucking the flame into the paper, he felt the tobacco ignite and warm his lungs. He closed his eyes to keep smoke from watering his eyes. The spring of their junior year at their tiny Midwestern high school, Lew and Janine had been sweethearts voted "Most Likely to Live Happily Ever After" at the Spring Banquet by their class of 12 fellow students. No one could have foreseen the events that would separate them following that school year. Her mother had died suddenly of a suspected aneurysm, and her father had decided to uproot his only daughter to move closer to family in California. There Janine would finish her senior year of high school.

Lew exhaled and took a step forward to retrieve the retreating smoke a second time into his lungs. Tears burned his eyes. Despite his love for basketball, Lew had foregone his senior season and graduated at semester. There was no commencement; he simply didn't return after the fall session. He planned to beat Uncle Sam to the punch and enlist before he could be drafted. It wasn't idealism or romantic notions of war that compelled him to act. His own father had served in the Great War and had shared stories of mustard gas and trench warfare. A Purple Heart rested in a velvet box atop the bureau in the dining room. No, Lew had been ready to move on with his life, and military service stood in the way of getting on with those things, namely his life with Janine.

He settled back against the olive drab monolith as the heady rush of nicotine subsided. Lew and Janine had written regularly at first, even if she sent three letters to any one of his. She poured her heart out by the page. He factually recounted details of his daily life, although she sensed deeper emotion underlying each basketball score and account of chores done. If he didn't exactly wax eloquent, he did devote several short sentences to odd jobs he accepted to pay for a second-hand car and to help his folks. Lew took another long drag, the cigarette burning his fingers.

Lew pitched the butt to the ground and blew smoke through his nose. He nodded and smiled as Sgt. Haywood, their

119

commander, told the gunner, driver, and ammunition loader about a time his hounds treed a racoon in the middle of an ice storm. Lew had heard the story before. "Greased Palm," Haywood looked directly at him, "those dogs were baying and sliding all over the place." His name was already short. Lew wondered at their longer name for his ease in loading shells, hitting each with the butt of his hand as he did. The Army had way of twisting the name for everyone and everything. He laughed with the others, each of whom had his own issued honorific--Alfred Morgan or *Jeeves*, the driver; James Oak, a gunner whom they dubbed *Oakley*, which he protested was a girl's name, and their commander, Sergeant Ralph Haywood, whom they called "Hey Would You Stand Me a Drink" but not to his face.

Pinching a loose piece of tobacco from another unfiltered Camel from his tongue, Lew gave the appearance of joining in their camaraderie, but his mind was on a stash of letters. Although he couldn't bring all Janine's letters to the

European front, since arriving Lew had amassed a sizeable stack of correspondence that he bound together tightly with twine to conserve space. Janine's last letter, the one he knew his buddy Dale would call a John Dear, rested in his breast pocket behind the soft-pack of Camel straights.

As the smoke break came to an end, the crew attended to the routines of life about the tracked vehicle they called home. Lew conducted his ordnance inventory. She would always love him, she said. From her earlier letters, Lew knew that since her mother's death, Janine's father had remarried, and the new stepmother had made it very clear that she was not willing to share her home with any reminder of her new husband's old life or former wife. A daughter was foremost among the unwelcome remnants. As Janine had graduated high school, the new Missus thought it not unreasonable that Janine be expected to contribute to her livelihood. This meant finding a job and lodging elsewhere. Janine secured a position in the office of a shipyard that had a government contract and found an apartment nearby, which she shared with two other girls.

The tank began to roll, pitching over the uneven terrain. Janine didn't have to remind Lew of their last time together. She had seen Lew in person only once since moving to California and that was right before he left for basic training at Fort Knox, Kentucky. He had driven over a thousand miles from the Midwest to California, Jerry cans of water lashed to the running boards, as he crossed the desert. The water was added twice as often as gas. Lew and Janine had shared three glorious days in the sun before he left, leaving the keys to the newly paid off car and his heart with her. Lew and Janine had waved to one another until the departing train was out of sight of the station. A week later he reported for his induction into the U.S. Army.

Lew tried to catch some sleep against the constant jostling of the armored vehicle. He'd grown used to its rough cadence.

Ten days after completing basic training, Lew shipped out from New York and arrived in Liverpool another ten days hence. Following a brief stay in Le Havre at Camp Twenty Grand, a staging camp so named after a brand of cigarette, Lew had the miraculous good fortune to meet up with a friend from back home. Dale Coleman had dropped out of school to enlist, too. Lew, Janine, and Dale would have comprised a full quarter of their graduating class had they remained together until the spring of 1945. Now commencement exercises would go on without them.

Despite the fitful nature of sleep in the confines of a shared space with four other men, their noises and their smells, Lew was thankful he wasn't still on foot. Together with hundreds of newly arrived troops, Lew and Dale had marched 109 miles within the first three days of their arrival to find their place on the front row of the European theater. Blistered and numb from the cold, Lew and George billeted for a time in the home of the Marchand family who had a beautiful if

123

willful married daughter. Mireille was the wife of a soldier who was away serving his homeland against Vichy encroachment. Lonely and bored, she set her sights on Lew, who steeled himself against her uninvited attentions with thoughts of Janine. Dale teased that his girl would never be the wiser and that Lew should live a little before he died forever on the Western Front during the coldest winter on record.

Lew had worn Janine's perfumed stationery close to his heart to protect him from Mireille's advances. Now he carried her letter telling him goodbye. During that layover in the French home, his feet, raw from the merciless trek, formed calluses in time for him to receive his assignment as ammunition loader with the 28th Infantry which took them toward the Ardennes Forest.

Lew had fended off amorous overtures under the protection of paper and ink. Genuine U.S. Steel-plated armor and artillery protected him against incoming mortar rounds during their sojourn through the Ardennes. Still Janine's letters had sustained him, continuing regularly as they had amidst the irregular mail calls of nomadic life. A fanfare of wolf whistles and feigned faints marked each hand-to-hand delivery as soldiers sniffed envelopes addressed in a feminine hand.

Lew's dispatches, never as frequent, lengthy, or as passionate as Janine might have liked, had grown even less so as the distance between them increased. Time, space, and experience made the young lovers' separation more pronounced. Lew lacked the words to adequately express the brutal experiences of his winter trek through the bitterly cold Ardennes, which she took for a cooling of affection.

As Lew, Dale, and thousands of others faced the brutality that was the Bulge, Janine agonized under the West Coast sun and waited for the mailman, who began to take a shine to the curvy brunette by the letterbox. One day the postman, an eligible fellow named Rudy, spoke to Janine as he reluctantly handed over onionskin correspondence postmarked U. S. Air Mail. Rudy had received a deferment as a sole surviving son, he explained to Janine, so he remained on the home front doing the important work of delivering the U.S. mail. Lonesome as she was in her shared beachfront bungalow, Janine found his attentions flattering. He lavished her with gasoline rations and nylons. When he unexpectedly proposed, and she just as unexpectedly accepted.

Realizing she had a car of her own which might suggest an independence of mind, one she might change, Rudy insisted they marry before a justice of the peace post haste. There you have it, Janine wrote, ripping the bandage off with little fanfare. She was Mrs. Rudy Edelman now and there was no going back. Her tone softened as she admitted that she hated that she was breaking Lew's heart. She was heartbroken herself. Then her tone stiffened again as she wrote this letter

126

would be her last. Rudy would not take kindly to her continued correspondence with a GI overseas. She was going to try to hang on to Lew's letters to her, few as they were, but she asked him to dispose of any letters from her. It would be easier that way she promised.

Huddled in the belly of the tank, Lew figured she was right. There was nothing further to be said, and Lew was not about to write again, knowing Janine's husband handled his letters. The first chance he had, Lew touched his Zippo to the stack of letters tied with a string and tossed them on a smoldering ash heap.

He didn't have much time for second thoughts as his crew chased retreating Jerries across the thawing landscape toward Leipzig. A year earlier, Lew and Janine had been feted as a couple at their Spring Banquet. Early blooming tulips and daffodils had adorned the tables. There would be no banquet or jonquils this spring, only K-rations and mud. Life was clocked in hours of boredom tinged by minutes of anxiety punctuated by seconds of seemingly unending terror. Lew's greased palm automatically loaded rounds of mortar fire as rapidly as they could be spent. Designed as anti-aircraft artillery, enemy flak guns fired back with equal effectiveness against the Allies as anti-tank guns. For days Lew fed the machine that ate through the Nazi defenses. Following a weeklong battle for Leipzig, the 28th Division captured thirty-five Nazi 88mm flak guns.

Heralded as a great feat, the munition capture and subsequent capture of 365 German prisoners of war proved a Pyrrhic victory for Lew. Under heavy panzerfaust, as Lew's tank evacuated wounded American soldiers, his buddy Dale, an infantryman, became one more casualty of war. Hit by small arms fire, Dale was taken prisoner in Leipzig at the Battle of Nations Monument where Napoleon had likewise faced defeat. A stronghold of the Third Reich, the granite fortress served as Hitler's SS high command post. When the monument fell under the relentless siege by Allied artillery, retreating SS and captive US troops alike were entombed in rubble.

The relentlessness of war drove the 777 deeper into the Rhineland. In the days following the fall of one of Germany's most powerful and populous cities, Lew's battalion rolled up to the fenced enclosure of Leipzig-Thekla in the grey dawn. Inside the gates, the battalion discovered a Buchenwald subcamp housing nearly 1500 concentration camp inmates. Emaciated human shells, along with the remains of those whose time ran out before their rescue, were liberated or buried by Allied troops who discovered them in the waning hours of the war.

According to the discharge papers following his honorable separation from the United States Army a year later, PFC Lewis Palmer received two Bronze Stars, an Overseas Bar, an American Theater Ribbon, a World War II Victory Medal,

129

a Good Conduct Medal, and $174. 70 for his service in Rhineland Central Europe. When Lew arrived back home, an official looking envelope with the White House as the return address awaited him. Signed by Harry Truman, the letter of appreciation read: *To you who answered the call of your country and served in its Armed Forces to bring about the total defeat of the enemy, I extend the heartfelt thanks of a grateful Nation. As one of the Nation's finest, you undertook the most severe task one can be called upon to perform. Because you demonstrated the fortitude, resourcefulness and calm judgment necessary to carry out the task, we now look to you for leadership and example to further exalting our country in peace.*

Lew returned home safe and relatively sound, but as the President had suggested, his work was not over. There were more lives to save.

The Family in the House with the Terrace on Hawthorne circa late 1950s

Every Friday night, after she was paid, Dazy took the city bus from her new job at Houston Feed to Green Hills Market for groceries. Zane waited as she completed homework, 8th grade math, her least favorite subject, in the living room. The Jules Street bus stopped at 31st and Sylvanie, five blocks west of their house on Hawthorne, so Dazy hauled two brown grocery sacks the rest of the way home. As Dazy's road back from hepatitis was even longer than that trek, their week's worth of grocery items was dictated by her arm strength and determined by her budget. Most nights Dazy and Zane split a broiled minute steak, plain baked potato, and boiled vegetables. Gradually the pallor of Dazy's skin and the whites of her eyes returned to a more normal hue of chalk white, but she remained rail thin.

Zane's vantage point by the picture window allowed her to

see Momma as soon as she came into view carrying the week's haul. In winter, the street lights were already on by the time Dazy reached home. Zane would put on her coat and slip on her galoshes as she waited to dash down 46 narrow terrace steps and race down the block to help carry the sacks of canned goods, produce, and cheap cuts of meat back up the 46 steps to the house. Fortunately, the milk man delivered dairy. The duo might not have owned a car, but they had been able to keep a roof over their head, and a dog who now enjoyed full range of the furniture.

One February twilight before Zane could station herself in front of the window, Nosie began to bark. Dazy walked through the door with only her purse over her arm. She held the door open for a genial gentleman bearing two sacks of groceries. Nosie continued to bark, but Zane was too stunned to quiet her. Dazy led the man into the galley kitchen, where he deposited the bags and turned to her daughter. "You must be *Noisie*," he said over the dog's barking. The women shushed the spaniel. "And you're Zane," he said softly,

wiping his hand on his work dungarees and holding it out to

Zane. Dazy prompted, "Zane, this is Lew from work."

Dazy had mentioned names of people who worked with her

at Houston Feed, but it had never occurred to Zane that they

had lives outside of her mother's work. After an

uncomfortable hesitation, it occurred to Zane to take the

extended hand, and Lew shook it appreciatively. Then he

bent down to scratch Nosie behind the ear. Her barking

ceased. "Lew gave me a lift after work," Dazy gushed as she

hurriedly put away groceries. "He took me to Green Hills. In

his car." Dazy sounded as amazed as if he had taken her to

Mars in a spaceship. Before she could stop herself, Zane

dashed over to look out the front room window at the yellow

and black two-door hardtop parked at the foot of the steps.

"I'd like to invite you both out to supper," Lew stammered.

"If you don't already have plans, this being Friday night and all." He looked at Dazy. "Maybe we could go to Snow White." Dazy looked at Zanc hopefully. As if they ever had Friday night plans. Zane shrugged. The nonchalance of her demeanor masked her excitement.

Dazy and Lew's first date was a family affair. Zane's presence made talking slightly more awkward but allowed Dazy to even consider his offer at all. The three of them sat in a red booth, Dazy and Lew seated on the bench opposite Zane. Lew handed Zane nickels to play the tabletop jukebox. When "Blue Suede Shoes" came on, Lew stabbed two forks into crinkle fries and put on an impromptu Charlie Chaplin meets Elvis performance. Dazy laughed and laughed, and Zane liked this kind man on her behalf.

The following Friday brought a repeat of the previous week, without the stunned reaction, barking, and introductions. Lew drove Dazy to Green Hills and brought her home with groceries. They ate hamburgers and fed nickels into the jukebox at Snow White as Buddy Holly and the Crickets serenaded them. Zane doodled on a napkin with a ballpoint pen. A caricature of Nosie driving a '57 Chevy, paw resting on the door of the open driver's side window, and a cartoonish scene of forks, fries, and ketchup bottles swing dancing emerged. Her attention was focused on her cartooning, but she hearkened to hear Dazy and Lew's conversation. As they left, Lew pretended to twist the lid on the salt shaker loose, and Dazy batted his arm. He took a flat toothpick out of his shirt pocket and put it in his mouth, explaining he was trying not to smoke as much.

The next Friday, Lew and Dazy brought home three sacks of groceries, and Lew volunteered to help Dazy cook. As Lew and Dazy cooked, Zane put away groceries. She had no idea where to put the small box of flat toothpicks at the bottom of a sack. "Oh, those are mine," Lew said, taking them from her. For a bachelor, Lew was handy in the kitchen. He said he often ate breakfast for dinner, especially SOS. Zane looked perplexed so Dazy explained to her that SOS, creamed chipped beef over toast, was an Army euphemism for "sh*t on a shingle."

The days grew longer, and Lew brought over a small charcoal grill and briquettes one Tuesday. After they ate grilled hot dogs and potato salad, Lew rolled up his sleeves and washed dishes as Dazy dried. He offered to help Zane with her math homework but was as hopeless as she was when it came to new-fangled algebra. He explained that he hadn't quite finished school, and Zane did some calculations in her head to realize he was several years her mother's junior. But he was clearly crazy for her mom, and Momma clearly grew more smitten with him each time he came over.

Zane knew exactly when her mother fell in love. One spring day they came home to find Lew lowering a lawn mower down the terrace and pulling it back up with a rope. They didn't even own a lawn mower, so the yard was already tragically overgrown by April. Zane considered the many ways in which Lew had tossed them a lifeline, as she and her mother trimmed shrubs with kitchen shears. Later, the three of them went to Dairy Queen for malts, Dazy's treat. Lew gave Dazy a sip of his chocolate malt, and Dazy gave Lew a taste of her strawberry one.

When Lew stopped in front of the house on Hawthorne to drop them off, Dazy stayed in the car as Zane climbed the terrace stairs. The street lights came on as Dazy told Lew about her family. Starting from the oldest, Dazy enumerated her brothers and sisters, counting her siblings on her fingers. Each had red hair like their mother.

Dazy told Lew of her beloved dad, a hard-working farmer who had died years earlier. Dad was not a perfect man, but he was a loving father, and she missed him terribly. Theo Reuben Wakefield had kept a journal throughout his adult life. She, too, kept a daily diary. If she took after anyone in her family, it was her dad. Also like Theo, Dazy had black rather than auburn hair like the others. That distinction set her apart from the first. She was the black the sheep after all.

Within the confines of the darkened car, Dazy told Lew about her Mother, Enid, who doled out more vitriol than affection, usually dripping in ink. Mother had moved off the farm and into town, but as she lived out of state, they didn't see her often. Distance kept them apart even when they were in the same room. Her mother Enid took pride in the purity of her pedigree, while Dazy felt humiliation that her Mother considered inferior any whose heritage was more melded. Zeal and righteous indignation characterized her mother, who, Dazy explained, fought for prohibition and the vote for women. Dazy told Lew of her mother's involvement with the Women's Christian Temperance Union but couldn't bring herself to confide her mother's darker alliances with associations committed to disenfranchisement, discrimination, and outright persecution.

Dazy explained her failed marriages and the personal difficulties those dissolutions created. Lew already knew Dazy had financial and health issues, but Dazy disclosed that she had experienced mental and emotional ones, too. She had so many regrets as a mother. Truth be told, there were times their mother-daughter roles seemed reversed. Once after she had lost her job, Dazy had borrowed money from Zane, whose father sent her occasional checks, to make ends meet. Dazy had paid her daughter back with interest so she could buy the Schwinn she had been saving for. Dazy told Lew briefly about her marriage to Zane's dad, Johnnie, and about her short-lived one to her former employer.

As the night grew late, she apologized for monopolizing the conversation and asked Lew to tell her more about himself. His folks lived in a small town and ran a feed store, and his sister was married with two young daughters. He liked to joke with his nieces. He mentioned that like most every guy his age, he had served overseas during the war. And, he added, he had once had a steady girlfriend.

That night when Lew Palmer returned to his one-room apartment, he unloaded his pants pockets as he did at the end of each day and placed his keys, change, and billfold on the bureau. He picked up the wallet and removed a folded envelope he had carried with him, out of habit more than anything, since his Army days. The inked return address was entirely faded, but the fragile onionskin letter inside was still intact. He didn't re-read it. He knew its contents by broken heart. It was the only remaining contact he had with Janine, as at her request, he had burned her bundled letters somewhere along the European Front. This one he had hung onto for the return address, but the only record he had of her married name and place of residence had entirely worn away. He dropped the envelope, letter still inside, in the trash, turned off the lamp, and turned in for the night.

140

Over the next several weeks and under Nosie's supervision, Lew made some improvements to both the front and back of Dazy's place on Hawthorne. He added a hand railing to the terrace steps in the front and broke up the concrete of the patio in back, replacing it with patterned brick. Dazy talked Zane into donning her black and white wide-striped pajamas and holding a sledgehammer in the middle of the busted-up patio. Zane was embarrassed to be dressed like a chain gang criminal for a picture, but she humored her mother because she had never seen her so happy.

Dazy's once sharp and angular features began to soften and fill in. When Lew bought not one, but six heart-shaped boxes of Russell Stover chocolates for Valentine's Day, Dazy put up a mock protest. "I gotta couple of kid nieces and my Mom and Sis and Zane," he explained, blushing. For a fleeting instant, he thought of Janine and hoped Rudy Edelman was buying her flowers.

As Zane's own father Johnnie had once made an impression taking her to school, Lew and Dazy now made one by dropping her off at sock hops after picking up a couple of her girlfriends along the way. The new plaid blouse with pearl buttons from Townsend and Wall at 6th and Francis gave Zane confidence, and she couldn't help but feel proud as the yellow and black '57 Chevy parked curbside at Bliss Junior High for them to pile out. Even the popular kids thought *Bliss* an ironic overstatement for any building housing teen-agers. While the adolescents mingled at the dance, the couple would stop in at the Frog Hop or the Hawk and listen to live music and jitterbug for a bit before picking up the girls at the end of the evening.

The courtship continued, the dynamics of the two-member family shifting to admit a third. In time, Lew rebuilt the terrace wall, the one that had collapsed years before, pushing Dazy over the precipice. When Mr. and Mrs. Palmer married late in the summer before Zane's freshman year, Lew gave

Dazy a wide white and yellow gold band, art-carved in milgrain scroll. No diamond, no separate engagement ring. Dazy had worn those before. This ring would last for a lifetime.

"A Kiddley Divey Too, Wouldn't You?"

Becoming Zanie

"Zanie, how on earth can you possibly have an *I* in English," Norma asked in astonishment. "You're the best student in the whole class."

"I didn't do the book report," Zane admitted.

"What? You read all the time. You even told me you were up all night sitting in your closet with a flashlight reading," Norma reminded.

"I couldn't very well do my report on *Lady Chatterley's Lover*, now could I?" Zane said.

"Your mom's gonna scalp you. You always make straight Es. I have an S, and you're way better than me. Bev, what do you have in English this quarter?"

"An M," Bevy sighed, not looking up from the Monopoly board. Bevy chewed on her braids.

"I love to read," Zane said. "And write for that matter. I just despise writing book reports." She popped the adapter out of the 45 on the record player and put it in another record. Crackling filled the air until "Hit the Road Jack" came on, and the girls started singing, "Now woman, oh woman don't you treat me so mean."

"You didn't have to write one, Zanie, just turn one in. Why didn't you reuse one of your old reports?" Norma shouted over the music.

"I can only report on *East of Eden* so many times. I re-used the one I wrote freshman year in Mrs. Swarthmore's class sophomore year. I was afraid I'd get caught. Those teachers talk, I just know it."

"I saw that!" Zane exclaimed as Norma swiped a $50 bill from the game's bank till.

"You caught me fair and square," Norma confessed, returning the blue bill, plus a green one. Their rules permitted cheating as long as no one was caught, then it cost the offender an extra bill from the next lower denomination. If the cheat didn't have the correct change, she had to fork over an extra sawbuck.

Bevy might not have excelled at schoolwork, but she knew how to cheat. She bragged she had once kyped three $100 bills in a single game--one from Zane's treasury and two from the bank--without the others' notice. Her strategy was to keep her money in a messy pile, rather than the neat stacks organized by denomination as the other two did.

"Are you girls studying for your psychology test?" Dazy asked through the closed doors.

"Yes, *Mother*," Zane said just as the other two chorused, "Yes, Mrs. Palmer" in unison. Their laughter led Dazy to believe otherwise.

"We probably do need to study," Bevy conceded quietly, eyes crossed as she inspected and nibbled off her split ends.

Zane pulled out the three-ring binder from her red plaid satchel to test the others. "Okay, what's the psychological term for the ability to recall images from memory over time?" she quizzed.

"*Photographic* memory?" Bevy asked, her answer logical but incorrect.

"*Idiotic* memory, you dunce," Norma said.

"Wrong, *eidetic* memory," Zane corrected.

"Sometimes I think I have more of an *Etch-a-Sketch* memory," Bevy conceded. "If I shake my head, it disappears."

"If I really want to learn anything, I work better alone," Norma said, pulling out her psychology textbook and turning to the chapter review questions. Bevy sat on the twin bed reviewing her notes. With Nosie's head resting on her lap, Zane looked over her notes and began to sketch in the margins. The girls had met at freshman orientation when they had each registered to be on the Outlook, Central High School's newspaper, staff. Zane had received recognition at Bliss Junior High for her artistic ability and was assigned to draw editorial cartoons. Norma signed up to write, and Bevy loved photography. The girls suggested Zane needed a name for her cartoons. "How about Plain Zane," Zane offered, but the editorial staff overruled her suggestion, dubbing her recurring lampoon of student life *Zanie Zingers*.

Fellow students soon turned first to the mimeographed page that featured the comic strip that flowed from Zane's pen. One week featured a caricature of classmates who had worked together on a campaign for 10th grade class president. In successive frames, Zanie, as she was becoming, depicted the true story of fellow students making a giant banner with permanent Magic Markers on someone's kitchen floor. Students on either end of the banner worked toward one another coloring in the three-inch wide lettering. When they picked up the completed banner, the letters "S-O-P-H-M-O-R-E" were not only misspelled on the banner, but the letters had bled through the paper and were indelibly imprinted on the kitchen linoleum. In the last frame, a father holding a briefcase remarks, "Wise Fools" to the mother sobbing at the table, the missing "O!"

hovering above her head in the caption bubble.

Thus, *Zanie* stuck as a nickname for the *Zinger's*

creator. Zane feared it conferred a degree of frivolity

and fun that she wouldn't be able to live up to, but

Norma and Beverly sought to prove otherwise.

Norma envied Zane's given name and said it was

even better than her nickname. Norma hated her own

name and wasn't overly fond of the great aunt for

whom she was named. "She's normal, ordinary,

regular, medium, average, you know, Norma!"

Beverly actually liked her real name and resented

being called *Bevy* from childhood all because her twin

brother, Beryl, couldn't pronounce Beverly correctly.

Norma and Bev began Zane's induction as Zanie by

showing her how to launch a roll of toilet paper

underhanded while teepeeing a yard. Together they

149

placed cellophane over toilets in the girls' bathroom. Their exploits brought out a side of Zanie that the first fifteen years of life had not cultivated.

Together the girls joined Pep Club as freshmen. Their squad uniform was a blue wool pleated skirt, which they rolled at the waist band to make shorter, and a white sweater with a Central Indian logo. One of their unofficial cheers was, "We must, we must, we must increase our busts. The bigger the better, the tighter the sweater, the boys are depending on us." Saddle shoes were mandatory, but Zanie wore white tennis shoes and took the demerit for being out of uniform.

Also as freshmen, the three pledged Lambda Alpha Lambda. In those days, Hellenic life started at the high school level. During initiation, Zanie had to dress as a peacock and stand in someone's yard. Her sorority sisters applied peanut butter to 50 tiny ponytails on Zane's head. Zanie cried as Dazy used Tide to remove pasty peanut spread from her scalp. "Be glad it wasn't the chunky kind," Dazy consoled when Zanie considered quitting. "I've learned indecision is harder than inconvenience so make up your mind," her mother advised. Zanie figured she had it better than Bevy, whose own mother was removing Black Jack gum from her daughter's braids, and she had already weathered the worst, so she stayed, vowing to be kinder to the next year's novitiates.

As Y-Teens their junior year, the three wore pastel formals and held both teacups and borrowed teacup poodles dyed to match their dresses as they road in the Apple Blossom Parade on the float they had stayed up all night stuffing with tissue paper. Zanie's lavender dress matched Gidget, the diminutive dog on her lap. She would have rather held Nosie, but the spaniel's colors clashed with the pastel theme. Norma and Bev, in pink and green, matched Fifi and Lucky respectively.

By the time they were seniors, their bond was forged by a shared history of adversity and experience. "I'm starving," Bevy said yawning, her braid falling from her opened mouth. She stretched as she stood. "Let's go to Wade's for chili." The girls argued whether Miller's Grill or Wade's Indian Grill had the best chili. They reached a compromise: Miller's had the best tenderloins, but Wade's had the best chili. They decided instead to head downtown to either the Victory Cafe or Maid Rite, depending on whose cars might be parked outside.

Zanie cupped Nosie's head in her hands and gave the spaniel a kiss on the head. "Let me change real quick," Zanie said to her dog and her friends. She switched out her school clothes into her usual attire, faded Levi's and a green short sleeve sweatshirt. She kicked her discarded clothes into her closet and slid it shut. "Stupid doors," she muttered as the sliding door slipped off the track for the bajillionth time.

"How much money do you have?" Norma asked Bevy, who started to count her stack of Monopoly bills. "No silly, real money."

Bevy emptied her coin purse on the bed and counted. "Eighty-three cents," she said.

"We're loaded then," Norma concluded.

"Hey, Lew, can I borrow the keys to the Renault?" Zane asked sweetly. "Pretty please."

"I don't know," Lew teased. "Maybe you should ask your mother." Lew and Dazy had still owned the yellow and black '57 Chevy with a manual transmission when, at the 22nd and Mitchell intersection, Zanie had practiced at the wheel with Norma a front seat passenger and Bevy and Dazy seated in the back. "I don't think we've covered how to negotiate red lights on a hill," her mother remarked as the car rolled backwards into the car behind. Zanie had nearly failed her operator's test the first time, having taken the driving portion of the test in her visiting father's new baby blue Ford Mustang. She had turned on the windshield wipers when asked to turn on the lights of the unfamiliar vehicle.

Lew tossed her the keys. "We'll be careful," Zanie promised as they headed out the door and down the terrace stairs to the new white five-speed Renault.

154

The girls punched the radio button to tune in WHB. Zanie planned her route strategically. As they passed Shanin's Drug Store on Messanie, Bevy said, "Hey, let's get an ice cream later on." Bevy was always hungry. They stopped at the level intersection for a red light at 22nd and Messanie by the just-opened Sears store where she had practiced driving in the newly paved parking lot. "Too bad you can't order a driver's license from a Sears Roebuck catalog," Zanie mused. To avoid parallel parking, Zane parked curbside three blocks from the diner.

Finding no one they knew at either location, both within walking distance, the girls settled on steamed loose meat burgers and crinkle fries from Maid Rite. The girls divided another order of crinkle cut fries between them. Zanie thought about the time Lew had re-enacted the Little Tramp's fork and potato dance at Snow White to "Blue Suede Shoes." When Bevy fed the remaining coins into the jukebox, Zanie made a microphone of forked fries and Bevy and Norma belted along with her to Jan and Dean's version of "Barbara Ann." Even Bevy, who ate the potato props when they finished, was too full for a chocolate ice cream cone.

On their way home, Norma pointed out the open window and joked, "Hey, there's Zanie's stop sign!" Once on their way to a slumber party following a football game, Zanie, Norma, and Bevy met up with four older girls as they walked to Norma's home around midnight. As a practical joke, the four girls, seniors, decided to depants Zanie. They held her down, removed her Levi's and took them to the corner stop sign at 26th and Mitchell where they tied the jeans to the signpost. With the help of Norma and Bevy, Zanie, thankful that her short sleeve green sweatshirt could be pulled long enough to cover her underwear, had disentangled the denim dungarees.

Bevy and Norma laughed to remember that night. Even Zanie, in hindsight, could see the humor. The more her friends laughed, the funnier the situation seemed to Zanie, who turned a corner too sharply. The little white Renault tipped onto two wheels and before Zanie could right it, the car toppled over onto the driver's side. The girls lay in stunned silence save for the crackling of the radio's off-station reception.

"Are you guys okay?" Zanie asked.

"I am," said Norma.

"Me, too, I think," Bevy agreed.

Norma managed to climb out the open window from the passenger side and reached in to pull the other two out. They gazed blankly at the little car lying on its side. The unscathed passenger side shone brightly in the midday sun. "Why didn't you just prop open the door?" came a male voice. The girls turned to see two handsome young men walking across the street to assess the situation.

"Need a hand?" the other asked. "On three." Together the five of them lifted the little car, which bounced as it landed on all four tires. All were surprised and the girls especially relieved to see that the damage to the driver's side was minimal. The girls drove slowly and without the radio the remainder of the way home. But not before giving their telephone numbers to Robbie and Ted, the two boys who had come to their rescue.

"It's a boy," Dazy whispered to Zanie that night, holding her hand over the mouthpiece as she turned the telephone over to Zanie. Norma and Zanie had debated for hours the following Saturday over what to wear on their double date with Robbie and Ted before settling on pencil slim Pendleton pleated skirts dyed

to match their sweater sets and pointy toed high heels.

Bevy helped in the wardrobe selection but didn't feel

at all left out as she had been going steady with

Clarence Barlow since fifth grade.

The two suitors picked the girls up at the house on

Hawthorne. The four walked single file down the

terrace to Robbie's dad's Model A with a rumble seat.

As Zanie took in the fold out seat, Ted detected her

panic and offered to help her climb into the fold out

seat, no mean feat in her pencil skirt.

Arriving early for the seven o'clock showing, the

boys bought tickets at the movie box office window,

and the couples browsed in the five and dime next

door before smuggling roasted nuts into the Trail

Theater. The girls were sure the heavenly aroma

would give them away when the usher tore their

tickets. The boys purchased Cokes in waxed cups with paper straws at the concession stand. Then they promptly poured their peanuts into the soda pop, an action Zanie found to completely nullify the point of warm roasted nuts. The house lights dimmed and the opening sequence of Alfred Hitchcock's *Psycho* began. As the movie reached the crescendo of the shower scene, Zanie hardly noticed that Ted had put his arm around her shoulder.

Life Continues

Zane balanced the weight of the diaper bag on one shoulder against the chubby toddler hanging opposite before using the handrail to ascend the 46 steps. "One of these days, Grandpa and Grandma Lew are going to live on a level lot," she groused in a singsong voice to the children as she followed the little girl climbing one step at a time ahead of her. Saturdays Zane

brought the kids by for a visit while her husband Ted

slept, having worked overnight at his factory job.

Stopping halfway, Zane took a breath and waited as

Lew bounded down the steps toward them. Meeting

them halfway, he reached for both children. "Do we

ever have something for you!" he said, giving both

kids a quick peck on the cheek. "Hi, Zane," he added

over his shoulder as he turned to take steps two at a

time upward.

Grateful for the lightened load, Zane followed Lew

and the kids to the top. Only then did she remember

she had left the letter from Daddy in the tiny

Karmann Ghia. She tossed the diaper bag onto the

redwood deck that Lew had built fronting the house

and headed back down the steps.

Returning, Zane followed offkey voices singing the jingle of a hotdog commercial into the family room. "I have news . . .," she started, "Daddy's coming for a visit." She stopped. Lew and Dazy were gently bouncing the two children on a huge red vinyl inflatable package of hotdogs, a marketing novelty from Dazy's job at Armour, a packing house in the Southend. And they were singing a commercial jingle: *"Hot dogs, Armour hot dogs, What kind of kids eat Armour hot dogs?"*

"Fat kids, skinny kids, kids who climb on rocks," sang Dazy, whom the kids called "Grandma Lew" as a counterpart to "Grandpa Lew."

"Tough kids, sissy kids, even kids with chicken pox, love hot dogs, Armour hot dogs," Lew ended in an exaggerated finish, *"The dogs kids love to bite!"*

Lew looked over at Nosie, who lay on a throw rug. Her legs stretched out behind her, joints up, giving her what they joked looked like a Cadillac rear end. The spaniel shifted position, curling inward as if to express her annoyance with the festivities. The kids giggled as they jiggled atop the giant bounce toy. "Hotdog, hotdog," the little boy chanted, wishing to sing the jingle again.

"No, let's sing 'Mairzy Doats,'" requested the girl, who loved the zany sound of the song her grandma often sang with them.

"What on earth?" Zane shouted over the toots of toy wiener whistles that accompanied the cacophony.

"Your mom got 'em at work," Lew breathlessly explained of the inflatable bounce toy and shrill whistles.

"The perks of the job," Dazy laughed. Dazy had the distinction of having been promoted from secretary to purchasing agent, the first female in her company to ever hold the position.

"Grandma Lew has some great news," Lew said to the children.

"What's your news?" Zane asked.

"No, no, you go first, honey," Dazy said. "When is your dad is coming?"

Zane unfolded the letter she had brought from the car to verify the date of his arrival. "Friday night. He'll be here over the weekend. Now, what's your news?" Zane asked.

"Why don't you all come to dinner," Dazy suggested.

"Sure, thanks, but what's up?" Zane persisted.

"Oh, it's not much," Dazy said, downplaying the importance of any announcement on her behalf.

"Not much?" Lew echoed incredulously. "I have a something that proves otherwise." He held up a framed certificate, dramatically cleared his throat and began to read, giving special emphasis to each word. "'Be it known that Dazy Palmer is hereby commended for groundbreaking excellence as a Purchasing Agent.' It's signed by Who's Who of American Business Women," Lew added proudly.

Zane hugged her mom. "Good job, Mom. Congratulations," she choked, her voice muffled in her mom's neck. Her mother had always been a pioneer, at one time yielding disdain as a divorced mother raising a child on her own and now earning praise as a trailblazing business woman in a world of men.

"Yay, Grandma Lew!" chorused the kids, who had no understanding of the significance of what had occurred or any idea of the magnitude of their grandmother's recognition.

"Guess that gets Grandma out of the doghouse for beating me at rummy," Lew said, wiping his eyes as he removed the personalized dog cut-out from within the wooden doghouse plaque and hanging it on an empty hook. A little dog with each of their names, including Nosie, hung from a peg. "Who's in the doghouse next?" he asked. "Me!" each of the children shouted.

The night of Johnnie's arrival, a shiny red Mustang pulled up to the Palmer residence, the blended family assembling for a cookout at the house on Hawthorne. Zane's husband carried the little girl, Johnnie carried the little boy, and Zane carried potato salad and baked beans though the house to the patio. Dazy and Zane brought side dishes from the house to the picnic table as Lew manned the barbecue grill. After dinner, the boy played on a wooden car, turning the steering wheel on the car his Grandpa Lew had built. With help balancing from Grandpa Johnnie, the little girl tried to walk on stilts Lew had made.

Grandparents shooed the children away from a girl's bicycle leaning against the long ago re-constructed back terrace wall. They didn't want the heavy bike to topple over. "Is that my old bike?" Zane asked incredulously of the formerly red and gray Schwinn from Western Auto that she had saved up to buy. The bike was now a shade of house paint blue. "Yep, my nieces wanted to freshen it up a bit," Lew remarked. "Did it themselves. Can you tell?" He laughed.

As the sky darkened into night and lightning bugs did their aerial dance, the kids caught glow worms and put them in an empty mayonnaise jar with holes in the lid. Johnnie smoked and offered Lew a cigarette. "No thanks," Lew said, "trying to quit."

Johnnie lamented the rising cost of cigarettes and regaled them with stories of buying cartons of cigarettes from the commissary in the Army for the price of a pack these days. He had kept the officers he chauffeured well-stocked, and they paid him handsomely. Always one to make a buck, Johnnie's generosity managed to turn a tidy profit.

Johnnie told of how he had seen Bob Hope in a USO show one time and lamented the disappearance of Big Band leader and Army Major Glenn Miller over the English Channel. Johnnie continued to regale them with all the celebrity acts he had seen during his time in the Army. "Hey, weren't you over there for a time?" Johnnie asked Lew.

"Yeah, for a bit," Lew answered, turning to ask Dazy if he could give her a hand with the cleanup.

"That would be great," she said, rising. As Zane watched, her children dragged the inflatable hot dog package to the backyard to use as a launching pad to leap into the air at fireflies, it occurred to her she had not seen the spaniel. She followed her folks into the house looking around. "Mom, where's Nosie?"

169

Lew and Dazy stood in silence in the kitchen, looking at one another. Lew answered to spare Dazy. The vet had had to put Nosie to sleep, he explained, the aches of age and pain of arthritis had caught up with her. They had put her out of her misery for fear she might snap at the children. The women cried, accepting the necessity of the decision but knowing the special role the little dog had played in their family through the years, the stability that four-footed friend had provided. "I wasn't nearly this sad when Mother died last month," Dazy said, blowing her nose.

"Doc said she'd have been about 90 in dog years," Lew offered in consolation through tears of his own. "Probably had over a hundred thousand miles on her," he added with a wry laugh. "Not sure how well the U. S. mail will continue in her absence."

On their way home, Zane looked out the window from the backseat of the Mustang, her dad as ever the chauffeur. She felt guilty for having been so preoccupied with her children and her own concerns that she had not noticed Nosie's absence earlier in the evening. She wondered if there was a heaven and, if so, if there was a place where all creatures, great and small, go when they died.

That night after Ted left for his midnight shift, and the kids and her dad went to bed, Zane was unable to sleep. She went into the kitchen and quietly assembled her art supplies. She settled on pastels, to which she had graduated from water colors during high school. She sketched a magnificent lion lying in a field. At its side, she outlined two reclining figures. With white and Payne's gray pastels, she quickly added the wooly texture of a lamb against a blank area in peripheral green grass. She spent considerably more time shading the black and tan markings of the cocker spaniel opposite, legs outstretched behind it. The coat glistened with softness when she finished. She didn't understand exactly what it meant, but somewhere she had read that one day the Lion would lie down with the Lamb. She had made room for Nosie, as she once had for her imaginary friends.

As in Life, Death, late 20th century

Zane refolded the letter from her father, addressing her as he always had, as *Zane Elizabeth*. She gleaned his most recent residence from the hastily scribbled Las Vegas return address on the envelope. She pulled out the contents of the envelope, a letter, a check, and a sunny yellow postcard. Daddy had often included postcards, but this one, spelling in neon lights his residence at the Daisy Motel, was a revelation. Zane

172

wondered if her father's life had begun with Dazy and now would likely end at a pay-by-the-week motor inn called the Daisy Motel. That his address, Room 21, on 415 South Main, was on the Vegas strip caused her to shake her head wryly.

Like his father before him, Johnnie sought opportunity. His forebears had crossed the Atlantic; he crossed the country. Sometimes opportunity took a female form that he chased, even in his senior years. For a time, he had thrown his lot in with the heir to the Neiglick family, a daughter he married after her parents and older brother were long gone. She didn't have to change her name from Neiglick when they married or revert to it when they divorced. Johnnie remained a nomad at heart, and the urge to retire in warmer climes suited for year-round golf led him first to California, then to Florida, and now, Zane surmised, to Nevada. Wherever the grass was greener or the sunshine more affordable, Johnnie had followed the allure of unexploited pastures.

"We all die of something," he had written. The check he had included was for $135. His life savings. As a postscript, in red, he had printed in all caps, "CASH THIS CHECK AS SOON AS YOU CAN." Throughout his daughter's life, Johnnie had written often, visited on occasion, and sent checks when possible. Though at times he'd joke, "Charge it to the dust and let the rain settle it," many times Daddy's checks were all that kept Zane and Dazy from homelessness. And now he was admonishing her not to waste time before cashing this one.

From her childhood, Daddy had shared sage advice of questionable appropriateness. When he took Zane to the Arlington Park race track as a child, he would explain his system of placing bets based on the appearance of the horse owners' wives. If the wives were in attendance, their hair neatly coiffed or they were attired in finery and a fancy hat, that was a sure sign they expected to be photographed in the Winner's Circle. Sometimes his system even worked.

Now he was dying. The letter outlined the "kemo" protocol, as he called it, at the VA hospital. He marveled that his nurse was "a Lieutenant Colonel by rank. You would never guess." She looked "just like a regular nurse." Despite her rank, he wrote that "Nancy" was about Zane's age and very efficient. He wrote that his blood was lavender, a medical oddity that baffled Zane. Following the update on the progression of his grave health concerns, he wrapped up his letter and his affairs, concluding "Keep me in your prayers."

From her earliest days of fearing that through prayer she might let something slip that an omniscient being had overlooked, Zane had matured spiritually. Her earliest conception of God had been shaped by others, namely Dazy's rejection of her mother Enid's dark fundamentalist outlook. Whereas in her later years Dazy sought truth in reason, moderation, and even meditation, Zane, it can be stated no other way, had found Jesus. Or rather, she was wandering through life seeking purpose, and He found her.

Until her middle years, Zane had only a vague notion of a judgmental God who was distant at best and disapproving most likely. By embracing a Christ whose unconditional love overlooked the imperfections that had kept her on life's periphery, she found a Savior who also loved her, accepted her mother, and could allow each to forgive her grandmother. Though she personally might have preferred that Enid baste in a brimstone cauldron such as the one into which she cast others, Zane found freedom in forgiving the old lady and encouraged Dazy to do the same. Enid's eternal destination had already been determined and was out of their control anyway. Continuing to live under anyone's toxic influence, she decided, only poisons those who continue to partake. Poison you ingest can hardly be expected to kill anyone else, and especially not those already dead.

As Dazy and Zane had forfeited precious years of their life to that woman, Zane endeavored to cut her losses and willed her mother to do likewise. In this way, Zane continued to love her mother toward heaven. Now her Daddy, Momma's first husband, was asking for intercessory prayer. Whether he asked as a trite benediction or an earnest plea, she intended to honor his request.

Prayer had become a constant in Zane's life. One time she was asked to teach a Sunday School class. She felt ill-equipped and unqualified but accepted the position because the need was there all the same. So, she prayed and worked and studied to prepare and show herself approved. Had someone told eleven-year-old Zane she would one day lead prayer and Bible Studies for other women, Zane would never have believed this possible. But belief had become the hallmark of her being. Still, her mind occasionally strayed as she spent time in prayer, and now she wondered if Daddy was still alive. The letter's postmark was the previous Tuesday. She considered who might notify her when the time came. It likely would not be anyone she knew, perhaps the police or a landlord or, maybe Nancy, the Lieutenant Colonel.

"I'm thankful for a good life, so kiddo, don't worry. One day at a time from here on out," he'd written. By the standards of most, Zane's dad's idea of what constitutes a good life left her thankful he could see it that way. Born to parents who passed through Ellis Island on their way to greater promise, Daddy's immigrants found nightmare in the American dream. Zane's middle name, Elizabeth, was an homage to the woman who had died saving her children in a long-ago Chicago tenement fire. Both of her grandmothers, Zane realized, had had a hand in shaping her. One in disdain, the other in sacrifice.

Zane considered that despite early odds, she had achieved a good life by the standards of most. For one thing she was still married to Ted. That was proof there was a God. They had eloped young and stayed together through the inevitable turmoil of marriage. They stayed together for the kids' sake and managed to mellow into another decade of marriage. The blessings of faith and family buoyed her, and the artistic talent she had developed as a solitary youngster sustained her emotionally and fiscally. Sales of her wildlife paintings proved profitable enough to help her own children pay for college.

Zane re-read Daddy's letter before bed. Then, like every night, she prayed for her father. Zane considered that being speechless before God was not unlike her father's living selectively mute before authorities as a child. Now rather than fearing she might inadvertently bring divine wrath down on her parents at any reminder of their plight, she prayed God's blessings on them. She asked for her father's well-being, beseeching her Heavenly Father for the healing of her earthly one. She prayed both of her parents would find peace and soul's rest.

Zane took her Daddy's inclusion in his letter of a Biblical promise, "By His stripes we are healed," to be a hopeful sign. She recalled times in her life, and her mother's, when Scripture references weren't so inspiring.

Within weeks of Daddy's letter, Dazy called her daughter to tell her that a certified envelope addressed to *Zane Elizabeth Neiglick* had come to her address. The use of her maiden name, in care of the house on Hawthorne, made it a wonder Zane received it at all. Maybe the use of her middle name, a reminder of a grandmother she had never met and a mother that Zane's own father barely remembered, had worked as a talisman. The letter had been sent from the Clark County coroner's office in Las Vegas.

Zane told her mom to read the letter to her over the phone. Hearing the not unexpected second-hand news of her father's passing, Zane Elizabeth remembered she had not cashed Daddy's final check. Instead she had put it back in the envelope with his letter, tucking both in the copy of *Twenty Million Tons Under the Sea,* by Daniel V. Gallery, the senior Al Neiglick's autographed copy of the book Daddy had once given her for safekeeping.

"I'm so sorry, honey," Dazy consoled Zane in the loss of her father, adding that she had long felt remorse that Zane had had to grow up in a broken home. Their divorce had set into motion events and regretful situations that Dazy could never have foreseen. If she could trade places with Johnnie in death and in so doing wipe away any suffering, loneliness, or alienation Zane had experienced due to their separation, Dazy would do it, do it over differently, in a heartbeat. "That's not how life works, Mom," Zane comforted her mother. "There's no such thing as a do-over."

As for her own pain, Dazy reflected she wouldn't change a thing now. Her life with Lew was the happiest she had ever been. Zane agreed. They had only really become a family when Lew had entered their lives. Lew not only salvaged their family but made Johnnie feel welcome to play his part if he happened to be passing through. Now Johnnie had passed through for the last time.

Zane thought about her heritage, the traits passed down by each of her parents. Even as a child, Zane had favored her father in appearance. Any artistic ability, though, came to her from her mother. Zane spent her days painting wildlife scenes. Many of her oil paintings sold at art shows and helped finance her children's college educations. Dazy, who as a young girl had filled her room with pencil sketches of

Hollywood stars, turned to quilting in her latter years.

Every stitch, even the quilting, was done as a labor of

love by hand. She created quilts that would become

treasured heirlooms for her daughter and

grandchildren. Each square had a significance, a tie,

to the intended recipient. Dazy hoped the quilts would

be a lasting legacy.

As in time her health declined, Dazy had one last

request of Lew, who unbidden remained at her side to

the last. The October following her death one

September, wrapped in one of her mom's quilts, Zane

watched from the window as Lew raked leaves into a

pile and set them ablaze. He then fed handfuls, page

upon loose-leaf page, of narrow-lined notebook paper

on the pyre. From her first days in Chicago, Dazy had

kept a record of her life, much as her father had. As

for Lew, this was not the first time he had carried out

such a request, sending the words of a woman he loved up in smoke. Fearing her mother's voice lost forever, Zane longed to read the journal entries but stayed inside as Lew burned each unread word. Though Zane wondered what might have filled all those three-ring binders, she had no doubt her mom had been proud of her.

She hugged the quilt more tightly. Given the chance, Zane would be more attentive, offer more support, focus less on her own concerns and more on others. "Everyone feels that way, honey. But even you said, that's not how it works," Zane sensed her mother echo.

Now and Hereafter

I met a woman recently, yes, though few and far

between, apparently there are others here. Attractive

gal, lively, and quick to laugh. I guess "lively"

wouldn't be the right word. Anyway, as we seemed to

be fellow sojourners, and there being few others with

whom to speak, I decided to strike up a conversation.

"What are you in for?" was my feeble attempt at

humor and opening gambit. Fortunately, she shared

my warped sense of humor. "Mesothelioma," she

quipped, "Lung cancer. Never smoked a day in my

life though. Exposure to asbestos in the 1940s caught

up to me. You?"

I joked that I hadn't lived long enough to die of old

age but that I had managed to outlive my body. I

mentioned that had I still been alive, I'd be 100. "In

human years," I added, hoping she was a dog lover.

She was. We talked about fur babies we had loved,

marveling how a silly mutt could steal your heart.

186

Talking about dogs was common ground, the weather

no longer being an issue for us. We worked

backwards from there, talking about our great

grandchildren, our grandchildren, and our children,

or in both our cases, child, singular. She had a son. I

had a daughter. Her son was a very successful

businessman. My daughter was a talented artist. Even

beyond the grave, parents brag about their offspring.

Figuring I had little to lose at this point, I was upfront

about my background and my marriages. I didn't see

the point in using names, but I was surprised at my

own candor. I told her about my parents and about

the men in my life. I told her how I recalled my final

words, calling out as I did for my daughter and then,

as I lay dying, my husband's name. He'd been my

third. You might think that would be haunting,

recalling how you cried out someone's name, but it

had been comforting. He had been there to the last,

loving and soothing me with his presence. He had been my rock. He had come along and saved my daughter and me. I told her how he had a generous heart, always helping any who needed it.

She said her second husband was like that. She said she would have saved herself a lot of grief had she waited and married him the first time around. Saved both of them a world of heartache really. She explained how they had been high school sweethearts, but that the war that came after the one to end all wars had torn them apart. She had moved away and was too young and foolish to hang on to the one good thing in her life. The marvelous thing was, years and years later, after she had been divorced for decades and he was widowed, they had seen one another again at a high school class reunion. They laughed because neither had actually graduated with the class, but they had all attended school together. They had cried, remembering a fallen classmate. They had

so much shared history, even if it had occurred over a

half century earlier. It was as if the intervening fifty-

plus years had never happened. She was no longer

brunette and he was completely bald, but they

immediately recognized one another, and being

together made them somehow young again.

They married with both families' blessing and lived

very happily until her diagnosis. Seems even working

in the office of a shipyard thousands of miles away

from the actual war could kill you over time if

asbestos is in use. He had been with her to the end,

too, comforting her.

We agreed we were each immensely fortunate to have

found such a soulmate. We both remarked how when

it came to what's important, life generally works out

as intended and offered no do-overs.

Neither of us knew what the future, If that's what you

would call it, would hold, but decided we could each

use a friend to keep company.

Author's Note

For years I wanted to write about events related to family history, but I

put off starting because I didn't know where to begin, and there was so

much of diverse information. Fifty-plus years of living, fragments of

conversations, photographs and mementos convinced me these were

stories worth sharing. In the months and years leading up to the

centennial of my maternal grandmother's birth, I researched my heritage,

the unknown and known. First, I delved into the genealogical mystery that was my maternal grandfather. I scoured ancestry sites and visited the

National Archives in Kansas City for any trace related to his life. Next, I

looked back at my maternal grandmother's side, which was stacked with

a preponderance of documentation. I read my great grandfather's

published journal, *Grandfather's Diary: The Writings of Leo Benjamin*

Horner of Saline County, Nebraska, During the Years from 1903 to 1939

(Copyright 1987 By Ann Hoback Registered with the Library of

Congress, Copyright Office Printed privately for the descendants of Leo

Benjamin Horner). I'm so thankful for the labor of love that went into

typing and compiling decades of hand-written ledgers to preserve family

history. I found my great grandfather, my grandmother's father,

fascinating, and his diary, spanning 500 pages and 36 years, insightful. I

was equally delighted and astonished by some of the revelations therein.

Though I drew on the journal for inspiration, events or characters in this

story are entirely fictional.

Most of what I have written comes from sources closer to home, in time

and place. I had a third grandfather on my mom's side. In every way

other than genetic, the man who inspired Lew was our grandpa. Although

he never spoke of his experiences in Europe during WWII, he epitomized

the Greatest Generation. A small cache of pictures, news clippings,

military papers, commendations, medals, and a hand-written log were

discovered in a safe deposit box after he passed, revealing the extent of his front-line experience. We already loved, adored, and miss him; now we are awed by his service, amazed by his sacrifice, and humbled by his humility.

Even with all those divergent strands, the thread that unites the story turned out to be my mom. Her own account of family history chronicles recollections of her childhood and that of her parents, who inspired the characters Dazy and Johnnie. These remembrances, which were often painful, were set down for my brother and me and for our children, so that we might know and appreciate some of the difficulties of our forebears. As I was writing, she would send me fragments of memories and small details that helped bring Zane to life. The challenge was presenting a narrative that would be of interest to others. My family is not famous. We do not merit the inherent curiosity of those whose lives are infamous. That means any story told as truth would need to be sold as fiction. In his recent novel *Varina*, which I started reading just this week but have yet to finish, Charles Frazier refers to those who write memoirs as struggling "to make themselves sit alone at a desk every day and conjure their version of history from the weightless tools of words and uncertain memory." So it is with the weightless tools of words and uncertain memory that I undertook this project.

Slowly a method of organization took shape, gathering momentum faster than I could type. I began drafting in my head even if I wasn't writing. I would dictate into my phone as I drove, compelled on more than one occasion to pull into a parking lot to type up developments.

Eventually I found myself awake at all hours. There were days I stood at the computer in my pajamas until after noon. I would begin again after dinner and work late into the night, sometimes into the early hours of the following day.

Did you catch the part about me forgetting to eat food?

A long-awaited hold on a best-selling eBook or audiobook would become available through the library, but I could not focus on the story for the one crowding my head. Driving, dreaming, and walking have always been states during which my mind is most productive. I longed for longer days of spring so that I could walk outside. Not only did I desperately need exercise and fresh air, I welcomed what I knew would be uninterrupted time and pace in which to develop the story.

My nature is to dabble at lots of pastimes, picking them up and putting them down. This project I embraced wholeheartedly and committed to until I was committed or its completion, whichever came first. Originally, I released the resulting book in a serialized eBook format,

193

installments published a few weeks apart. I chose to release parts before completion for many reasons, not the least of which is I am impatient and impulsive. The main reason, though, is it was much easier to tell construct a story from different vantage points if I completed one point of view before moving on to another. Thus, the non-sequential order.

I dedicate my effort to my grandma and my mom and hope to bring them honor. Grandma lived the experiences I feebly tried to portray, and my mom not only experienced many of those same events first-hand as a child, but also shared the very personal account of their life together. Though presented as a work of historical fiction, this book also stands as a testament of my love and gratitude for my grandfathers. Both Johnnie and Lew are based on actual men real to me, and each played such a significant role in shaping us, Grandma, Mom, and me.

I also wish to note the massive debt of gratitude I owe to two friends and travel companions who made meaningful contributions. Kim Fowler not only paid careful attention to detail while ruthlessly proofreading, she encouraged and provided impetus to keep writing. She saved me from typos, garbled syntax, and sundry embarrassing errors, at one point noting, "This is what we English teachers call a dangling modifier." Both she and I taught high school language arts. Whereas she retired teaching English, I long ago moved out of the classroom and into the library. Any errors in this manuscript are on me because I failed to fix what she clearly

194

tried to bring to my attention. Cathy Green excels at looking at the big picture. She had a storyboard in her mind, and maybe on paper, that allowed her to say, "Wait a second, I thought you said. . ." on several occasions.

Last, I want to thank those who read *Mairzy Doats*. I appreciate you all—your patience with my unorthodox means of publishing and your gracious comments via text, email, and Facebook. A few of you even posted on Amazon. To those whose device didn't update as I had hoped during the digital serialization, I apologize but am ever so thankful you tried! Hopefully the paper version is universally accessible. One loyal reader printed out all the pages of a.pdf copy. I cannot adequately express the depth of my gratitude but wish to thank you all.

The title *Mairzy Doats* comes from the words of a song my grandma used to quote. It wasn't until I was an adult that I realized that what I took for nonsensical sounds made some measure of sense. Kind of like this story.

Glory Fagan

196

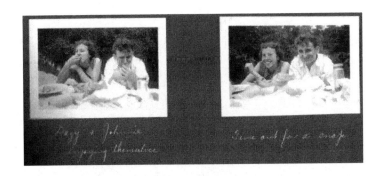

Peggy + Johnnie enjoying themselves   Time out for a snap

DAISY MOTEL
415 SO MAIN, LAS VEGAS. NV

Friday, 22: THE HOUSE ARRIVED at noon. Holis took E. to the train to go to [...] at noon. WE MOVED PART in p.m.

Saturday, 23: RAINED. part of the day. WE FINISHED MOVING.

October 24, 1926, Sunday: COLD. We went to Church to get warm in a.m. etc etc

Monday, 25: The two men pried the old house apart.

Friday, 13: That about ate my insides out. I got mighty sick & bloated.

Tuesday, 16: I took the girls to school and sent the Co. assessors paper in [...] plowed 3/4 of day, finished the east 8 acres plowing. We stretched the fence [...] pine trees. BORN WHITE CALF, Herby Hoover.

---

eshed the balance of the oats
field.) Then we threshed th
went to a K.K.K. meeting at S

---

left thus and went t
the ardennes forest

---

was ver [...]
we took the town of
Liebertwolkwitz. And
Then took Lipsig. [
Three day battle. a

and then went to the
company close to
Wurzenfelds. the next
morning we went up and
had to fire. that was on
sunday. we took 35.88 mm
guns. and 368 prisoners.

"Battle of Nations" Monument
downtown Leipzig, Germany, 19

In Leipzig
in 1945

To you who answered the call of y
country and served in its Ar
Forces to bring about the total defea
the enemy, I extend the heartfelt thank.
a grateful Nation. As one of the Natic
finest, you undertook the most sev
task one can be all 1

...demonstrated the forti-
, resourcefulness and calm judgment
necessary to carry out that task, we now
look to you for leadership and example
in further exalting our country in peace.

THE WHITE HOUSE

Harry Truman

Pictured are only a handful of the hundreds of photos and documents that served as research and inspiration for *Mairzy Doats*. Photographs include those of the author's family members upon whom the characters Dazy, Zane, Johnnie, and Lew are based, as well as excerpts from primary documents that inspired and informed the telling of their story as fiction.

Made in the USA
Lexington, KY
17 April 2018